Also by Mike Gipson:

Ocher's Dawn

Ocher's Rain

Ocher Jones Western Series
Book Two

Mike Gipson

This book is a work of fiction. Names, places and characters are the product of the author's imagination or are used fictitiously. Any resemblance to actual events or persons, living or dead, is coincidental.

Copyright © 2019 By Mike Gipson

Publisher – M.S. Gipson/KDP

All rights reserved. No part of this book may be reproduced or transmitted in any form or by any means without the written permission of the author.

ISBN-978-1-7321626-1-7

To Gayle

Through the Dawn of our almost fifty years,

enduring Rain, Wind, and Fire.

You've always been there.

Acknowledgements

Anne Armezzani, Judy DeCarlo, Janet Schwick, Lourdes Schaffroth, and Ann Vitale.

Ladies you continue to provide the insight and motivation for these books.

Thank You.

Anne Armezzani & Jim Brouwer

Without you two and all your guidance and encouragement, this endeavor would be in a drawer somewhere.

Characters –

Ocher Jones - Assassin, AKA Little Orphan, Traveler, named Shiilooshe by Ojos (Book 1), Ocher

Lewis & Amanda Livingston - Owners of the Double LL Ranch

Stacey Livingston - Daughter of Lewis & Amanda

Boyd - Owner of the High Range Ranch with an unknown background

Kemen Cortez (Baja) - Mexican Bandit who befriends Ocher

Tyler Gomez – Patron of the "Best horse Ranch in the West"

Holt Sturdevant – Texas Ranger

Shamus & Hanna Donnelly – Brother & Sister??

And a few more.

The Dawn

Ocher Jones, a trained Assassin, continues his attempt to escape his past. Searching for a future. His wanderings bring him in contact with the Good, Questionable and Bad of the Old West.

Trying to answer, *What do I want?*

Chapter One

Rain. It can be a help or a hindrance depending on whether you are the prey or the predator.

Tonight the rain is just plain annoying. For Ocher, there's no escape from the wet and cold. As he huddles inside his brand new, still-stiff poncho, the rain seems to find a way to creep in. Every once in a while, a cold drop meanders across the ceiling, drops straight down then migrates down the middle of his back and settles in the seat of his jeans. Rain wasn't what he expected when he rode into the sand mounds, arroyos, cactus and mesas of west Texas. But then again, he wasn't real sure what he expected.

He does feel right lucky to have found a small overhanging knob that affords just enough room for a fire and the coffee pot, but not much warmth. Occasionally the rain throws mud up on the coffee pot and it hisses as the spatter dries. Staying out of the weather requires total focus. The only saving grace is the coffee's hot and strong enough to make the dried venison chewable. It could be worse. The wind could be howling and lightning striking everything above knee high.

The Pinto isn't so lucky. Ocher knows his companion is used to the weather, but still. The Tobiano colored pony is responsible for finding the shelter. But he's now standing out in the rain underneath the tree, the only tree within sight. If you could call a sun-bleached, head-high scrub oak a tree.

Ocher moves the muddy coffee pot to the side, shifts his position to avoid the invading rain drops lurking, and settles in. The sound of the rain and the comforting squeak of a wind mill, somewhere out in the darkness, lulls him to the edge of sleep. The report of two high caliber rifle shots, about a second apart, intrudes on the solitude. He knows nobody should be out hunting in this rain, at least not hunting food. The shots are well spaced, deliberate, and fired from the same location - one shooter and no return fire. The rain may have just changed from annoying.

Now What? Since escaping from the Philippine jungle and landing in San Francisco, two years past, he's exercised all of his skills to adapt. Studying the people and learning the customs, constantly checking his back trail, changing directions, creating no patterns, leaving no signs of his passing, have become second nature. Staying unnoticed has become a way of life, all in an effort to escape the past and move toward a new future. He doesn't know anybody here, so there's no logic in getting involved. It's almost dry under the small overhang and the coffee will stay warm for a little while. Besides, not much can be accomplished in these conditions even with his skills. *Probably someone's shooting at varmints of some kind. Not my concern. Rain.*

Horses are animals with keen instincts. They tend to know good from bad, right from wrong, at least that's been Ocher's experience with the Pinto. Ocher sees the painted pony react immediately to the rifle shots. The horse sets his ears forward, moves out from the protection of the tree, plods to the small overhang, kicks over the mud spattered coffee pot and looks the huddled, semi-dry, traveler square in the eye. It would appear that the Pinto's decided that, in a choice between standing under the only tree within one-hundred acres getting wet, or going to investigate the two shots and getting wet, is not a debatable decision.

"Nope, I ain't coming out there in the rain, you want to go investigate you go right ahead. I'll wait right here."

The glare intensifies and the Pinto, to accentuate his intent, kicks mud into the shelter accompanied by a chuff.

"You can belly ache all you want, I'm staying right here," the traveler says holding up a cup of luke warm coffee.

The Pinto invades the space, grabs Ocher's pant leg and drags him out into the rain.

With the coffee gone and now sharing the small shelter with a wet, anxious horse, Ocher accepts the inevitable. Apparently something is wrong and Ocher's companion feels the need to get involved.

Breaking camp and packing gear isn't practical since this is the only shelter available and a dry place might be needed. The traveler retrieves the saddle and saddle blanket from the back of the overhang. The Pinto sees this and moves out of the shelter, into the rain, so he can be saddled. The Pinto is eager to investigate the shots and quivers as he's saddled. Ocher and the Pinto move away slowly from the overhang, using the rain to mask their movement. Ocher has to make a decision. *Am I the predator or the prey?*

The report of the two rifle shots was northeast of the small camp, less than a mile or maybe a bit more. Rain depresses sound. At about half mile, not wanting to ride into no good, the well-trained predator and the Pinto stop, listen, move forward a few steps then repeat the process. The splatter of the rain covers the sounds of the rider and Pinto. It also slows the progress of the search.

"Careful, big boy. You know what I know." Ocher whispers, but the horse's calm, easy manner, confirm Ocher's own instincts. The shooter is gone. The rain has slacked off just enough to see a big horse, as big as one of the Belgium that Ocher saw on a farm recently passed. The reins drag the ground. Making a slow approach, Ocher notes nothing remarkable about the black horse other than his size. The animal appears to be well taken care of. A short Texas style braided rope hangs from the polished saddle, a rifle in the scabbard, but no rider. The horses nuzzle each other and then the riderless horse turns and walks directly toward a body on the muddy sand. The body is face down, just off the trail near a Yucca bush. From the positioning on the ground, this person isn't playing possum, waiting for the shooter to come in closer.

No reason to hold back, the horses haven't made any sign that they sense trouble. The big horse is walking slightly ahead, the rain masking the smell of blood. Ocher dismounts and leaves the Pinto a short distance away to act as a lookout while he approaches the wet, bloody body. Ocher runs his hand across the flank of the gelding, which allows Ocher to approach and examine the cowboy on the ground. There are two bullet holes in the back of the poncho. The cowboy moans as he's turned over and the bloody poncho moves aside. He's been shot in the back, no doubt with the exit wounds in his chest. No use trying to do anything in this rain and mud. Ocher moves the gelding into position and hoists the cowboy into the saddle.

The cowboy croaks, "Thanks." With a gasp, he makes a request, "My hat." Then he slumps and grips the pommel.

Tough breed these cowboys. Ocher makes a quick survey but can't see the hat. The wounded man is the priority. The hat will have to wait.

How this hombre makes it to the shelter is a mystery, but he stays aboard for the ride to the pitiful little overhang. The haven isn't much better than the rain but at least it's not in the mud. Ocher eases the cowboy from the big horse and lays him out of the drizzle as far back as possible. A lesson learned from another cowboy is to always keep the makings of a fire in a dry spot in your saddle bags. The valuable lesson is now put to use. Ocher grabs just enough of the dry tender from his saddle bags to start a small fire.

He fills the coffeepot with clean water from his canteen and sets it on the fire to boil. His other shirt, the clean one, will be used as bandages. The plate used sometimes for beans and bacon will have to serve as a bowl to rinse out the bandages. Now to care for the wounded cowboy.

The poncho doesn't seem to fit just right. He's an average-sized man, but it's a very big poncho. That gelding doesn't seem right for the cowboy either. That dilemma is for later. The two wounds are in the upper left chest by the shoulder joint and need a doctor's care. Ocher's simple knowledge tells him to clean the muddy sand from the wounds, stop the bleeding and get this cowboy to a town with a doctor. But where's the nearest town or doctor?

The two horses apparently see no reason to stand about watching Ocher. They slog through the mud, over to the oak tree, seeking cover.

The silence is broken. This cowboy is full of surprises. He chokes out, "Double LL Ranch, southwest, five miles." This cowboy has to know he's in trouble and makes the effort to tell Ocher where he wants to be taken. A town would be better, but the ranch will have to do.

The wounded man can't make it one mile much less five, but then again he shouldn't have survived this long. As tough as he is, this cowboy can't sit a saddle for five miles. The tree sheltering the two horses will have to be sacrificed. It ain't much but just enough to put together a rough travois. Drizzle and darkness aren't the best conditions for building anything. Using every stick in the entire tree, the cowboy's saddle rope, and his own ground blanket, he soon constructs the drag behind.

Ocher removes his poncho and uses it to keep the rain out of the wounded cowboys face. The small caravan is on the trail as quick as the wounded man can be loaded onto the travois. The gelding seems to understand what's expected and starts for home and a dry barn, with Ocher and the Pinto following close behind. The shooter hasn't been forgotten. Trust the horses. They'll sense if anybody gets close. Still, it will be a long ride in the rain, cold, and darkness, over rough terrain.

Chapter Two

The gelding leads the way home and the small band arrives at a ranch house. In the wet and moonless overcast, there's not much to see of the buildings. Ocher is soaked to the skin and both boots are full of water as he steps down from the Pinto. His every step squishes inside his boots as he moves onto the covered porch. The front door is substantial and set in very well, reflecting the care and craftsmanship used in building the adobe ranch house. He can see light emanating from the back of the house through a shuttered side window and smells the aroma of freshly baked bread. Ocher's efforts at the door finally conclude in the shadow of a lamp ghosting its way toward him.

"Who is it, and what do you want?" The question comes from one side of the door and not directly in front of it. Smart move.

"You missing a ranch hand?" Ocher cautiously responds.

"Why?" comes the reply, but from a different location from the first question. Real smart.

"Cowboy got shot and gave directions to here." The door opens immediately and a very big man in worn jeans and work shirt steps out with a rifle leveled at the intruder. The big man looks past Ocher toward the gelding with the travois attached. He's moved aside by a healthy nudge from a handsome, small, at least in comparison to the man filling the doorway, woman in a modest, homemade dress. She's holding an oil lamp in one hand as she wipes flour off her other hand onto her apron. Without hesitation she moves out into the drizzle, her hand held up to the chimney of the lamp as she approaches the travois. She moves the poncho aside to identify the wounded cowboy.

"It's Woody!" she gasps. Turning, she says to the big man, "Lewis, get him inside. Be careful." Then turning to a younger version of herself, who has just stepped out of the shadows, "Stacey, get some water on to boil and get some clean white sheets." She turns to Ocher and asks, "How bad?"

Not wanting to commit one way or the other Ocher responds, "I've seen worse." In an instant, the women with the pale blue eyes and Ocher make a compact. He lies and she knows it.

The lady holding the lamp fusses at Lewis. "Be careful," she cautions. The big man lifts Woody with ease and follows along behind the light. Lewis, with Woody in his arms, fills the parlor and, as they pass a side board laid out with a tea set, one of Woody's dangling arms sweeps two cups and a saucer toward the hard wood floor. Ocher's a half-step behind the procession and sees the china headed for probable doom. With the ease of a bartender setting a shot glass on a bar, he grabs the saucer with his left hand and one cup in his right. He places the cup on the saucer and then catches the other cup. Lewis turns back toward the hutch in time to see Ocher catch and set the dishes back in place. Lewis raises his eyebrows, taking a second look at Ocher. He makes no comment, just turns and continues on through the parlor to a back bedroom.

With care that's surprising, Lewis lays Woody on a clean, freshly turned down bed. Lewis doesn't need any help but Ocher helps as he's directed by the lady with the lamp. Quickly the oversized poncho is stripped from Woody and the make shift bandage is removed so a cleaner one can be applied.

Lewis is the man of the house, but this lady knows what needs to be done and just does it. Although Stacey can't be seen, no doubt her duties are being completed. Ocher's presence is accepted but no further duties are assigned, so he just moves out of the way while the doctoring is being done. Stacey, the younger version of the take-charge women, enters the room with fresh bandages and asks, "How bad is he?"

The take-charge woman reaches for the fresh bandages, looks at Ocher, and the compact is complete. With a calm voice, says to Stacey, "I've seen worse." She lies and he knows it. "We'll need Doc Simpson."

Lewis and Ocher are shooed out of the room as the two women administer the care that they've learned from being ranch women. Woody's wet clothes are removed and hit the floor in a pile, as Ocher and Lewis close the bedroom door on the way out.

Lewis leads Ocher into the parlor, lights another lamp and gives Ocher a good looking over. He sees a young man, twenty or so, slightly less than six feet, well-kept, clean-shaven, dressed in working clothes and dripping all over the parlor floor. The young man's eyes are the color of granite, and when they shake hands, Lewis is surprised. The young man's hands are like stone, not like his own hands calloused from hard work, but like a rock that's been in the sun. "The hands are out on the range, so I'll have to ride to town for the Doc. You're welcome to stay. The bunkhouse, well... you'll find it."

Ocher removes his rain-soaked hat and, with a firm but courteous voice says, "Mister Lewis, I've already been out in that weather. I can't get any wetter. No need for you to go out in it. Just point me toward Doc Simpson's and I'll get going."

Even with his short time in America, Ocher has met men like Lewis, men who have to size up other men, cattle, and situations very quickly. Lewis makes his judgment, "Due south, normally about an hour, a bit more tonight. First house you come to is the Doc's."

Ocher dons his slicker and moves to the door. Lewis stops him and sums it up pretty quick, "Thanks."

The rain in Texas is different from the rain where Ocher was raised and trained. This rain turns to drizzle, like now, but in the Islands, it just stops. Following the muddy trail toward town is much easier than in the tropical rain forests. Here the trail is flat and open, not closed in with vines, vegetation, and covered over by the canopy. A canopy that's infested with critters that bite, sting, and kill. Although there are critters here that can bite, sting, and kill, most of them are on the ground.

The Pinto takes to the trail as if he was born to it and only slows once when they're confronted with a rain swollen runoff. The mountain-bred, trail-wise pony takes to the ankle deep water with sure footed confidence. Like magic, a house materializes out of the drizzle. Ocher dismounts, drapes the horse's reins over a rail, opens a gate in the fence, and walks to the front door. A hand-painted sign confirms that they've found the right house.

The man answering the door shows no surprise at being awakened in the middle of the night. Doctor Simpson has the eyes of a young man still eager for a challenge, but with a body that can't keep up with his eyes. After a brief explanation, Doc says, "My buggy's in the livery along with the horse and bridle. Get the rig ready and I'll be right out." No wasted questions, sentiments or emotions. Ocher nods and thinks to himself, *I like these people and the way they go about the business of living. You can't teach class, you just have it I guess.*

The old mare's not as easy going about the adventure as Doc Simpson. She fidgets around, tries to bite Ocher, twice, and finally manages to step on his foot. Ocher doesn't win the battle, but the horse finally relents and when the Doc arrives, she's ready to go.

The trip back to the ranch is without conversation. The Doc and the mare have obviously made this trek before and without incident. Ocher, trailing the buggy, arrives back at the ranch house just as the soggy and dreary dawn begins.

Doc Simpson goes straight into the house to take care of Woody. After a long night, Ocher stands alone in the morning gloom, tired, wet, and for the first time in a very long time, with no idea on what to do next. The Pinto has also had a long night and needs some rest and feed. Leading the weary horse to the barn, he unsaddles the Pinto, brushes him then feeds him a mixture of grain and hay. After he wipes the saddle down and places it over a saddle rail, he returns to the front porch. Ocher unties the mare and tries to walk the horse and buggy toward the barn. The old girl doesn't show any interest in going into the barn. She pulls Ocher toward a stand of Cottonwoods. "Ok, ok. If this is where you want to be, this is where I'll let you be." He uses the ground anchor he finds in the buggy and walks back toward the house.

On the front porch he removes his boots, pours out the water, peels off the socks and, after ringing them out, wipes out as much water from the inside of the boots. Hanging the socks over a hitching rail, he thinks, *At least growing up barefoot was less trouble.*

Sitting back in the rocking chair just for a quick rest, he peers through the hanging gourds. Even the gourds show the practicality of these people. No fancy flowers but peppers, several varieties. The ranch layout shows the same practical sense. The positioning of the buildings is well away from the high ground to the west, making a long range rifle shot impossible, even for him. The wide field of vision and a lot of open ground makes it almost impossible to sneak up to the ranch. The main house and the bunk house are made of adobe, tough to burn. The only burnable building is the barn which is set downwind of the other structures, eliminating the chance of a fire spreading.

The big stand of cottonwoods next to the creek cuts the wind. The corrals are set downstream and on the desert side of the ranch. If the stock's released, a round up will be easier in the desert than the hills and mesas.

The way the front door is set in shows that the adobe is two-feet thick. No bullet could penetrate the walls and the adobe keeps the temperature in the house comfortable. A great deal of pride, planning, and hard work went into this place. The place was built with strength in mind. The place can and probably is being watched.

Yep, he confirms in his mind, *I like these folks, maybe someday.* His vigilance melts away in the presence of this place and these people, sleep is upon him.

Chapter Three

The smell of good coffee, in fresh clean air, makes a man feel alive and ready for whatever comes next. That smell is in the air. Ocher opens one eye, sees the younger lady with the auburn hair standing next to him. Ocher, exercising his well-honed mental skills recalls her name. "Good morning, Stacey." He pulls his outstretched legs toward him and leans forward in the rocking chair. Too late he realizes that his legs are too far back and in the act of standing almost falls on his face. Regaining his balance he manages an upright position, brushes his hand through his hair, shuffles his bare feet on the porch beaming with self-pride that he remembers her name and can speak to her and remain vertical.

"Morning. Coffee?" She asks grinning.

Ocher has spent years of physical and mental training learning to use weapons of all types, how to adapt to any situation, practicing tactics, patience and honing the skills of observation. He even speaks three languages. However, all of that's now forgotten as he struggles with the simple task of responding to the young woman standing before him.

He marshals all of his strengths, remains calm, takes the hot cup of coffee, and manages to squeak, "Thank you."

Having completed two remarkable and engaging pieces of conversation, he tries for another. "How's Woody?"

In one glance, this auburn-haired woman with her mother's eyes and her father's calm strength has unsettled his disciplined world.

"Mother and Doc Simpson are still working on him." Her shoulders drop slightly and her smile now is forced. The body language reveals all. She's very concerned. "If you're done wrangling that rocking chair, why don't you come in for some breakfast? Your boots are in the kitchen along with a clean pair of socks."

Ocher's concern continues. *How did someone manage to get close enough to get my boots and socks? Why was my first reaction this morning to brush my hand through my hair? I don't know.*

Two hours of sleep is plenty. He notes that the weather has turned into a glorious west Texas day, clean air, and a breath taking view. This day even starts with a bonus: an inside, sit down breakfast. *Can't remember the last time.*

About half way through bacon, eggs, grits and biscuits, Doc Simpson, Lewis and the lady from the night before come in. Again, straight to the point, looking at the traveler, Doc says, "You probably saved Woody's life by cleaning up the gunshot wounds and applying pressure to the bleeding." He turns, looks at the couple and says, "Before you ask, I don't know, so don't ask. Infection could set in, or some other thing we don't expect. Keep him warm, and if his condition changes for the worse send for me. It's out of my hands." Doc is gone, and silence fills the kitchen.

The take-charge woman, takes charge. "I'm Amanda Livingston. This is my husband Lewis and our daughter Stacey."

Ocher won't look at Stacey, remembering the first encounter, a bit afraid she might ask him a question.

Amanda refills Ocher's cup with coffee, "Thank you for bringing Woody home."

After a calming sip of coffee, "Yes ma'am," is all that seems appropriate.

Lewis, trying to restore the natural order of his world, asks, "And who might you be and how did you come to be out there?"

"Ocher Jones, I was camped out about five miles, near a wind mill, sitting out the rain, when I heard shots and went to investigate." Getting up with his coffee cup in hand, he leans against the door jam and says, "Don't mean to be rude but let me ask you a question. Was Woody riding your horse and wearing your slicker?" The air in the kitchen goes still and all the sounds of the ranch stop as the answer to the question hits the Livingston's.

Lewis's answer and his intentions are summed up in a word, "Boyd!" Before he can move to leave the kitchen, Amanda stops him.

"You don't know that!" The conviction in her voice does not reflect her statement.

Lewis stops and looks at her, "I'm going over there, and when I leave, I'll know for sure."

Trying to calm the situation, Ocher says "Maybe there's an easier way to prove it."

Lewis is a man who's conducted his life by a philosophy of action, but he asks, "How?"

Ocher sits back down at the table, "I don't know this Boyd, but I do know that whoever shot Woody thinks they shot you. You have an advantage. Why not stay out of sight and see what develops?" Rubbing his chin, he continues, "Besides, if you go to Boyd's, you are confronting him in his territory, not the time and place of your choosing. If it's Boyd who did this, prove it!"

Lewis remains motionless.

Ocher continues, "You've worked hard to get this ranch. Don't take a chance and give Boyd an opportunity to take it all away. If he's a bushwhacker, going to him in his territory, on his terms, is a situation where your chances of success are very limited. At least have some breakfast before you go out there and die."

The struggle in Lewis's mind is apparent in every mannerism, jerking the chair out from the table, sitting down with a thump and grabbing his coffee cup, spilling the contents on the table. He wants to go and face 'Boyd' but he knows Ocher's right in assessing his chances. When he makes his decision, it's obvious, "I'll have mine scrambled."

Breakfast resumes quietly, just polite talk with an uncomfortable edge to the conversation due to Woody's condition. No long term mention of anything or no further mention of Boyd. Ocher is curious about Boyd but doesn't ask. Finally Lewis stands, "Ocher, I'm going to need another hand around here, at least until Woody gets back on his feet. You interested? Dollar a day and board."

"I'll help where I can for the time being, but right now, I'm just passing through. No disrespect, but I'll have to say no," Ocher replies.

Lewis accepts the comment, looks at Amanda and says, "Well, I've got things to do. I guess you and Stacey are going to tend to Woody."

Looking at Ocher, Amanda says, "I was planning on going into Pine Springs to pick up supplies, at the store, lumber yard and the feed store. I shouldn't go, with Woody's condition and all. Could you go for me?"

Ocher considers, *Should I ask Stacey to ride along?* Too intimidated to ask, he replies, "I'd be glad to."

Lewis, now full of breakfast, wipes his mouth, downs the last of his coffee, and starts toward the corrals. He looks over toward Ocher, "You got quick hands but don't wear a gun." It was more of a statement than a question.

"I don't like them, so I don't carry one," is the reply.

"As you've seen, this is rough country. You might want to reconsider," Lewis responds.

Ocher remains silent. Lewis doesn't need to know, that the man at his table, has been trained to kill with anything, everything, and nothing.

Chapter Four

Ocher likes to have a purpose, be it small or large. He takes time hitching up the wagon with a matched set of mules. The mules seem excited about going to town, or anywhere for that matter. The pair just wants out of the barn and to get a chance to go for a ride. The Pinto watches the activity but makes no move toward the barn to be saddled. The mares in the coral have captured his attention.

The trip into Pine Springs is almost uneventful, but about half way into town one mule throws a shoe just after coming out of the overflowing creek. The mules, one limping, pass Doc's house on the way into town. *The place sure looks a lot better in the daylight with the garden and fence out front,* Ocher thinks as they pass. The blacksmith is easy to find, just by following the ringing sound of a hammer hitting an anvil.

"Morning," the blacksmith says, tipping his forging hammer as if it were a feather duster. Ocher notes that, if you had to picture a blacksmith, this is the guy. He's as wide as he is tall, not fat, just wide and with a smile just as big.

"Saw you coming up the street. Those are Lewis's mules," the blacksmith says, laying down his hammer.

"Yep," is the reply. "I'm going up the street to get some supplies lined up. Think you could get him shod?"

"No problem. Cash business though, be a buck," he responds.

"I'll pay you when I get back," Ocher answers as he moves toward town looking for the dry goods store.

Ocher watches and listens for news of the shooting as he arranges all of the purchases for the Double LL. No one asks about the doctor's visit. It's still early and the gossip hasn't made the rounds, yet. That's a good sign. Those who did this aren't the silent type, not for long anyway. They'll just have to brag. Looking up the street to the livery, Ocher notes two things: one, the mule is back in his trace and two, a tall unshaven man with boots that need polish, wearing clothes that need washing and mending, is looking over the mules. *Good news, something just developed.* Walking back to the livery, Ocher's intention is to ignore the stranger, inspect the blacksmith's work and leave.

The cowboy speaks, "Heard you had some trouble out at the Double LL."

Silence is a great weapon. It causes people to think too much, behave erratic, and make stupid mistakes. Ocher's well trained in the use of silence, and uses it now. He brushes past the tall cowboy.

The unkempt cowhand's not accustomed to being ignored. He reaches out with his right hand to grab Ocher's arm, with the intent of turning him around. Ocher reaches across with his left hand, applies pressure to the back of the cowboy's right hand, with his thumb in a fashion that refocuses all of the cow poke's attention on the pain in his hand. While all of the cowboy's attention is on his hand, he's walked backward and into a horses' water trough. The man splashing about in the trough wants to do something, but his hand doesn't work, and he's humiliated about what's just happened. Ocher continues to walk toward the farrier, pulls out a cartwheel, Mexican peso, and hands it to the big smiling blacksmith.

Still smiling, the blacksmith says, "No charge. It's worth a buck to see you dump him in the trough. I just hope it don't sour the water."

"Who is he?" Ocher asks.

The big wide man points with his chin, "He works for Walter Boyd, out at the High Range outfit."

"Thanks," Ocher says over his shoulder as he climbs into the wagon and goes to gather up the supplies. Thinking to himself, *Looks like Lewis was correct. Boyd may be the one.*

Chapter Five

The mules know the way back to the ranch so Ocher is just a passenger, arriving back at the Double LL about dinner time. The team heads straight to the kitchen door and stops. Ocher's distracted by the variety of aromas coming from the kitchen when he notices an older gent, with the typical bowlegged gait of a man used to the saddle, ambling over to the wagon.

The cowboy removes his work gloves and offers a hand that's just as weathered and leathered as the gloves. "I'm Buford Tillsworth. My friends call me Beaver."

Ocher holds out his hand but doesn't know how to address the man. 'Mr. Tillsworth,' is too formal, but to immediately use the nickname 'Beaver,' doesn't seem appropriate. After just a slight hesitation, he says, "Ocher Jones, I'm pleased to meet you, Tillsworth."

Tillsworth smiles, "Beaver, my friends call me Beaver. Let me give you a hand with those supplies."

They unload the wagon and lead the team into the barn, take care of the gear, and turn the mules back into the coral, where they were earlier that morning. The mules, with their heads down, droop-eared and sad-eyed, seem to realize that the day's adventures have ended.

Ocher and Beaver walk back to the main house to store the town goods.

"We best get out of the kitchen before Amanda comes in. She'll surely have us clean something. Sounds like the rest of the hands just rode in. What say we meet the rest of the bunch?" Beaver leads the way out of the pantry, taking a cookie from a plate on the table.

Next to one of the corrals, four men are gathered around a cook fire, drinking coffee from a large blue enameled coffee pot.

Ocher's been around enough ranches in his short time in the west to recognize top hands. A top hand has pride in their work and their appearance. These men are wearing well-worn clean, work clothes and polished boots. The saddles and bridles on the horses tied at the corral reflect the same attention, clean and polished. *These are cowboys.*

"Fellas, this is Ocher Jones." The men take a quick, appraising look at Ocher. They know about the events of the previous night and show their appreciation by surrounding Ocher, shaking his hand, more or less welcoming him.

"Ocher, the tall fella is Dolan France. The cowboy in chaps is Gaither Smitt. The one with the coffee pot is Douglas "Dusty" Vance and the youngster there is Vaughn Gould."

"Coffee?" Dusty offers.

Even with Ocher's limited experience with cowhands and their cooking skills, he knows that the coffee offer is a small test.

"Yep."

Dusty pours some into a cup and hands it to Ocher, who takes a drink.

"One of you boys got a paint brush? I'll start painting whatever you want with this stuff."

They all laugh.

"Takes a bit of getting used to," Dusty says, "Better to keep working than come over here and loaf and drink that stuff."

The coffee test complete, the easy cowboy talk begins. When Lewis comes out a little while later, the mood and easy manner doesn't change, but the coffee cups are set aside and the boys go about their work.

"See you met the boys. They offer you coffee?" Lewis asks.

"Yep."

"Did you drink it?"

"Yep."

"You're still upright so it must not have been up to their usual brew. Seen a new shoe on one of the mules. That blacksmith don't work for free. Let me pay you."

"No need, I'll take it out in grub. Amanda's cooking is a whole lot better than mine. I'll take advantage of it before I hit the trail." He doesn't mention the water trough.

Ocher helps around the ranch, pitching hay in the horse stalls in the barn, cutting wood, making it a point to stay away from the coffee pot. He's just about to start some leather work in the tack room when he hears the chow bell.

Dinner, a noon meal, takes place in a 'summer kitchen' as Amanda calls it. This slightly peaked open pole barn has no sides. A long table with benches sits in the middle. The summer kitchen is a few paces from the house kitchen and is shaded by the trees. With just a slight breeze it's quite cool. It's a simple meal of biscuits with ham in the middle. There's milk, sun tea, coffee and fresh baked cookies the size of saucers.

The gathering is similar to meals at Ollie's in San Francisco. Ocher's adopted family and the orphaned kids Ollie and Marta take in. The men around the table, just kids only bigger.

With good simple food and easy talk, he even manages to speak to Stacey without stumbling over his words.

"Stacey, would you please pass me another cookie?"

"You like them?"

"Yes."

"I made them."

Ocher knows the conversation should continue but doesn't know how.

"They're very good," is all he can manage.

This is why he left the old life of Ulila, Little Orphan, the Assassin, and has become Ocher Jones. He experienced this feeling of family at Ollie's but now it's a different story. Stacey.

There's always work to be done. When dinner is over, the hands get back to the business of ranching.

"Lewis, I'm going to take a ride and see what I missed last night. I'll pick up Woody's sombrero while I'm at it."

Lewis is finishing up the cookies but manages, "Supper is around sunset. Be careful. I still think you should carry a gun." Lewis looks at Jones and continues, "High Range is that way. You'll see soon enough where the name came from.

Woody's sombrero is just where it should be. The hat is simple, functional and well-used. The wide brim hats used in the southern desert areas are needed for shade, but are pretty ungainly in the mountains where a cowboy hat has a much narrower brim. Ocher drapes the chin strap over the pommel and continues the ride.

Ocher and the Pinto find a strategic location just below the top of a mesa to assess the lay of the land. High Range is exactly that, a ranch on a plateau located above and to the west of the Double LL. At one time, the spread had miles of grazing land and enough water to support grazing. If this is the Sterling Range, Able Jones talked about, it's more suited for horses than cattle. Only thing worse than trying to raise cattle there, would've been raising sheep. Now, even after the rain, the ranch is nothing but desert scrub.

The slight elevation change makes the Double LL more suited to cattle. Lewis' range shows he understands ranching. By moving stock around, managing the water and grazing properly, the Double LL is lush with grass and in full bloom.

An educated guess would be, now that the grass of the High Range is barren, Boyd just wants more grazing land and intends to take it from Lewis. Not wanting to create any problems, Ocher doesn't cross up the mesa of the High Range land. It's about an hour before sunset when he starts back toward the Double LL.

The Pinto's ears go up and he pauses, just a step, letting Ocher know they're not alone. Three horsemen are silhouetted on a ridge line. No self-respecting cowboy would be so careless. They split up. Two start down one side of the ridge, the other one starts down the other side. It appears from their actions that the watchers intend to have some fun with a lone cowboy. The trap is simple: one cuts off any retreat and the other two stop any advance. Three against one should favor the larger number.

Ocher reins in the Pinto, tempting the three men to come to him. Hanging the hat on a Saguaro, he throws a leg over the saddle. He waits for them to come in. They do.

The term "cowboy" can't be applied to any of these men. A cowboy has the quiet confidence that comes with doing a good job, without being told how to do it. A good hand takes care of his gear and himself. These men reflect the overconfidence that comes with just doing enough to get by.

After they surround Ocher, one cowboy rides in fast, while the other holds up short, about ten paces back. Ocher recognizes him. The man is dry now. He's folded his hands over the pommel, the top hand showing a bright purple bruise. His hat's tilted back, with a slight smirk on his face, shows he's anticipating the entertainment to come. The third holds his ground so no escape is possible.

The charging cowboy reins in at his comfort range, about six feet. "You were on High Range, and the boss don't like anybody on his range."

Ocher just sits.

The man glances down and notes that the intruder isn't wearing a gun. "We're going to teach you some respect for other people's property." He knows that Ocher hasn't been on High Range, but that's just his excuse.

Silence.

The cowboy starts to move forward to emphasize his point. Ocher also moves forward, kicking the cowboys' right foot out of the stirrup then pushing him out of his saddle. The man's horse shies away from the Pinto and whinnies in protest. During the fall, Ocher reaches for the cowhands' pistol and pulls it out of the holster. The riderless horse startles and runs away, the stirrups slapping against his flanks. The confusion allows Ocher to turn and face all three of the men. As Ocher aims the Colt between them, the man from the water trough is now smiling broadly. The other men just look shocked at being out maneuvered.

Ocher waves the Colt, "Dismount." The situation's in Ocher's complete control and they know it. They get off slowly. "Holsters over the saddle horns." Sitting steady, he adds, "Now scatter the horses. It's a long walk back to the bunkhouse, boy's. Best get started."

The cowboy on the ground stands up, in an effort to regain some dignity, he straightens his back, sets his feet, readjusts his empty holster, and with purpose in his stride, starts toward the High Range bunkhouse. The man from the trough turns slightly and tips his hat. They know they've been bested, and don't like it, but they acknowledge it. Ocher empties the Colt and throws it out in front of them aways. He doesn't want them completely defenseless. He retrieves Woody's sombrero from the cactus and places it on the pommel, and rides toward the Double LL, never looking back.

Chapter Six

Seeing the way the High Range is managed, Ocher finds the ride back through the Double LL range pleasant and reassuring. The day's winding down, and the recent rain has cleaned the air. The scrub brush, grass, and prickly pear are fragrant now that the dust has been washed away and the desert is starting to bloom. However, as the horse and rider arrive back at the ranch house, Ocher instinctively knows that something's changed. Death hangs over the ranch like a fog.

Beaver walks to the Pinto as they near the barn, "Woody died."

The man now called Ocher Jones has been around death before, mostly delivering it. The aftermath of what's left behind is not something he's experienced. All through his ten years of training, he was distantly aware that there are long-lasting consequences for others, such as family members, but never actually had to face them. These consequences are, for the most part, why he changed his name, and escaped. He can't help the Livingston's cope with Woody's death but can help in other ways. Now that he's experienced a "family," he feels the need to help.

There's some outside influence on the ranch. Lewis controls the day-to-day operation, but Boyd's influence seems to over shadow everything. There's some piece of information missing. If Ocher can get Lewis talking, maybe all of the facts will come out.

After taking care of the Pinto and his gear, he keeps clear of the family and the hands. He's not a part of the family. As much as he wants to help, Ocher won't get himself involved unless asked. These people are off their guard and vulnerable.

The smell of the coffee draws Ocher to the pot near the corral. He pours a cup. The coffee's been stewing all day and is as thick as tar. It would be easier to chew than to drink, but he needs the distraction. Sitting on the porch step, he considers what he knows. Boyd is not a cattle man. He has overgrazed the High Range. His hands, at least the one's Ocher's met, appear to be hands that no one else will hire. To continue in the cattle business, Boyd will need more grazing range. The Double LL, it would appear, is his choice. Boyd has to know by now that Lewis is still alive and that all of the Double LL hands are right here. Boyd can box in the Livingstons and control all comings and goings. There has to be more. *What's the missing piece?*

Lewis steps out the front door and leans against one of the support posts. "Hell of a thing. Woody was a good man. He just went out to check on that old wind mill. I was just about to set out when Woody said he'd go. You were right. That was supposed to be me." Lewis kicks imaginary dirt off the porch, pulls some dead leaves out of the peppers hanging in the pots, looks at Ocher and starts to speak several times, but can't seem to get it out. Moving over to the corral, Lewis draws a cup of coffee from the pot, tries a mouthful, spits the brew out and walks back to the porch.

Lewis takes the cup and dips some water from a hanging gourd, has a taste and sets the cup on the window sill. "I know how to fight what I can see. I understand how to fight indians, weather, hunger and cattle thieves. I want to fight something but I don't know who or what. Pretty sure it's Boyd. The law out here won't take kindly to my approach. You were right about me taking on the whole bunch. It'll probably get me killed, but not before I rid the territory of that bunch."

Ocher doesn't want to discourage Lewis from talking so he remains silent.

"I reckon you earned the right to know. Boyd and three other men, rough men, came into the range about two years ago, just after the war. The High Range was struggling, as we all were. The Sterling boys owned it then. Somehow that bunch of thieves got control of the spread. I don't know where they went or how, just one day the Sterling's were gone and Boyd had the ranch. He did buy some stock, but a lot of stock just started showing up with odd brands, well, stock I think was stolen."

Lewis steps back to the coffee pot, pours a cup, looks at the contents and tosses it out into the dust. "The three men he showed up with don't work the ranch. You don't see them much, except when trouble is brewing. The rest of his hands ain't much, neither. He grazed the range to death and then sold the beef to a drive headed to Montana."

The big man strides back to the porch, pours water on his bandana, wipes his face and reties the cloth around his neck. "He took that money, or part of it, and bought the local bank and my note with it. He's just called in the note with only 30 days' notice. That gives me 'til the first of the month to pay up. I guess he thought he could make a sweet deal for the ranch, with me out of the way. My whole life is in this ranch. I want to give this place to Stacey. I won't let it go easy."

"How much and do you have a plan?" Ocher says as he gets up off the step.

Lewis sighs and says, "Five thousand."

"That's a lot of money. I can help if you want it."

"Appreciate that, but as you said, that's a lot of money. Besides why would you want to help?"

Ocher sets down his cup of coffee, "Friend of mine pointed me in this direction. This friend knew the Sterling brothers. Kinda mentioned, that they're trying to raise cattle on a horse ranch."

"You got a smart friend. I told them boys the same thing."

"I intended to come here and dicker with the brothers, to buy that ranch and hope to find someone to teach me about raising horses."

"At least you're honest about not knowing how to ranch. Some of us are too hard headed and have to keep stepping in it 'til we learn better."

"Lewis, I know another man and he owes me some favors. A businessman, with money. You willing to sign another note for the money? He won't take advantage. My word on it."

"You seem to have some mighty good and wise friends, Ocher. Let me think on the offer. If you're serious about learning about horses there's only one man to learn from. A Mexican man, a friend of mine, down in Sabinos, Mexico. He's the best. I'll write you a letter of introduction if you want."

"I'd appreciate that. Want me to stick around and lend a hand where I can?"

"This ain't your affair, so no need. Let me talk with Amanda on the note."

Supper is..... not supper. The hands come in, pick up a plate, set it down and leave without eating. Lewis sits quietly at the head of the table, hands around a cup of coffee. Amanda busies herself with washing dishes, that don't look like they need washing and Stacey is drying them.

Ocher, sitting at the other end of the table, is at least drinking his coffee.

"Ocher, I'll sign that note. Can't be any worse off."

"Ok, where's the nearest telegraph office. One that Boyd doesn't control the telegrapher?"

"Hadn't thought about him controlling messages, but you're probably right. Fort Stockton would be the closest."

"How far?"

"Two days easy ride."

"I'll leave tonight, full dark."

Lewis is quiet, looks down at his hands, and furrows his brow, "You think we're being watched?"

"Wouldn't you be watching?"

"Yep."

Chapter Seven

Ocher takes refuge in the front porch rocker to grab a couple hours sleep before leaving. Ocher doesn't feel right about intruding on the ranch hands by staying in the bunkhouse. Let them grieve. There's no concern about being observed leaving the ranch. Not with his skills. Full dark should be around ten thirty. He should be miles from the ranch headed toward Fort Stockton by the time the moon rises at around two thirty.

The fragrance of desert flowers and lavender brings him awake. Stacey touches his shoulder and as usual deprives him of speech.

"Ocher, its full dark."

He stands, enjoying the dark, especially standing there with Stacey. "Thanks."

"Dad tried to saddle your horse, but that Pinto wouldn't let him. He gave up. Mom and dad are in the kitchen. Coffee's on."

Ocher follows Stacey through the house into the kitchen. The moment on the porch is gone, but won't be forgotten.

Amanda turns from washing her hands in the bowl, sitting under the small hand pump. "There was supper left over. I made you a poke to take with you. It might be better than cold biscuits and bacon." Stacey hands Ocher the bundle.

Ocher accepts the package, wrapped in a bandana. He turns and tries to look Stacey in the eyes, knowing that, if he does, breathing will become a chore. Finally, "Thanks."

Ocher and Lewis walk through the blackness toward the dim lantern light in the barn.

Ocher saddles the Pinto, loads the vittles from Stacey, and steps up.

"Keep everybody close in and safe. Don't worry about the note." He and the Pinto are gone before Lewis can say anything.

The ride to Fort Stockton is uneventful with only quick stops during the day for water, coffee and to rest the Pinto. At night camps, he enjoys the food in the bandana. The second bandana confuses him, the one at the bottom of the poke. The one neatly folded with the scent of lavender.

Sun is just setting the following day as Ocher and the Pinto arrive in Fort Stockton. The fort is more of a frontier outpost, with just barely enough mercantile shops to call it a town. Ocher wants to spend just enough time here to send a telegram to San Francisco. The response to the San Francisco telegram will undoubtedly unsettle Boyd.

Ocher can see the dry goods store and knows he needs to stock up with some food. Stacey's food package is diminishing but the lingering scent of lavender remains. Besides, Ocher has a hankering for some canned peaches. He approaches the left side of a wagon where an old man and young woman are sitting. A cowboy's leaning in and speaking to the Mexican girl. The girl's trying to push the cowboy away. Ocher reins the Pinto just enough to the left to brush the man into the side of the wagon. The girl sees the opportunity and slaps the cowboy, who steps back right behind the Pinto. The horse, needing no prompting, kicks the man squarely in the chest with his left rear leg.

Gasping for breath, the cowboy stands, "You did that on purpose, mister. Step down."

Ocher walks the Pinto to the hitching post, drapes the reins over the rail and saunters back to the side of the wagon, tipping his hat as he passes the girl. "Senorita, Senor."

Ocher walks right up to the cowboy, "You were saying?"

"I said you did that on purpose."

"So?"

The cowboy's demeanor changes abruptly, "Sorry, mister. My mistake. Shouldn't have been behind the Pinto."

"Apologize to the young lady before you go."

The cowboy takes a step backwards away from the knife pointed at his stomach and walks around Ocher, "My apologies, senorita." He turns and glares at Ocher and walks across the street toward the saloon.

The old Mexican man smiles at Ocher, "Gracias, Senor."

Ocher tips his hat again as he passes the wagon then steps onto the porch in front of the dry goods store.

Chapter Eight

It's a quiet night, no moon and plenty of stars. Ocher's ridden about an hour away from Ft. Stockton after sending a telegram and getting some supplies. He's just finishing up the larder, given him from Stacey and about to open a can of peaches, when the Pinto's head comes up.

"*Company?*" It's wild country and no need to take any chances, so he steps into the darkness to await his visitor.

A sweat-lathered horse materializes from the darkness. In the saddle, hunched forward, is a man. He looks up at Ocher. The man's face is bloody, his eyes almost swollen shut and his lips split. "They're right behind me. Please help."

Ocher steps up to the horse and eases the man to the ground next to the fire. "Who's right behind you?"

"No time. Please, help my sister. Take this mister, please." The man slips a piece of paper into Ocher's hand and passes out.

Ocher slips the paper into his pants pocket. He stands to retrieve his kit bag so he can clean the man's wounds. *This is becoming a habit.*

Before he can start dealing with the man, both horses look up. *"More company."*

Three men ride into the camp. A sturdy looking man with a full beard and hard eyes points toward the man on the ground. "There he is, boys. Throw him on his horse and we'll head on back."

"He's in my camp and here he stays. Ride on back to where you came from. I got a man to take care of and a can of peaches to eat." Ocher aims his comments toward the bearded man.

"He cheated me at cards. I aim to get my money back. No business of yours, so step aside or I'll move you aside."

"Mister, you can't move me aside sitting in that saddle. Step down."

"Enough of your back talk. I'm just gonna shoot you and take him."

Out of the darkness a voice, "I would not do that if I was you. As my compadre said, 'Step down if you have the nerve'." As a Mexican man strides into camp. Tall, tan, wearing a large sombrero hanging over his back, his coal black eyes reflect the firelight. His very presence commands attention. With his right hand, he's aiming a gun toward the three riders. His demeanor is calm, and the manner in which he holds the pistol reflects the fact that he knows how to use it.

One of the three men whispers, "That's Kemen Cortez."

"Some call me that. I am called other things as well. You going to step down?"

"I want no part of you, Cortez..."

"Senor, you will not have the pleasure of facing me. You will not get past mi amigo."

A grin appears out of the bearded man, "Him?" He points toward Ocher. "I'll step down just for the fun of taking him apart. Then we'll leave."

Kemen aims his remark to the bearded man. "You have been warned."

The man steps down and hands the reins to the cowboy on his left. The bearded man is no taller than Ocher but is heavier. Years of ranch work have no doubt toughened him and a few bar brawls have bolstered his confidence. He steps toward Ocher and throws a left fist straight at Ocher's face.

Ocher has spent years converting his hands into weapons. Ocher steps to his right, deflects the punch with his left arm, and with a closed fist, strikes the back of the bearded man's knuckles. Ocher's hands are like stone. The back of the man's hand is soft and the bones are fragile. They break.

The bearded man recoils but does not give up. He holds his broken hand close to his chest and moves to position his good hand. He feints a punch, anticipating Ocher will repeat his previous attack. As soon as Ocher moves to his left, the bearded man drops his hand to avoid the punch on the back of the hand. Ocher delivers a round house kick right below the bearded man's right ear. The man's eyes gloss over and he collapses to his left, the dust rising around him upon contact with the ground.

"Gentlemen, collect your friend and leave before mi amigo gets annoyed with you as well."

The two other cowboys step out of the saddle, drag their companion to his horse and hoist him aboard. They consider saying something before retreating but think better of it.

Ocher turns toward Kemen, "Let's see to him before we share those peaches."

Chapter Nine

"By the way, I'm Ocher Jones. I gather from our visitors, you are Kemen Cortez?"

"My friends call me 'Baja'. I would be pleased if you also called me Baja."

"Well, Baja, I'm Ocher. Let's take care of this fellow. You wouldn't happen to know who he is?"

"No, Ocher, only that he has been badly beaten. Are you going to read the note?'

"Later."

Baja looks around the camp and notices that there are two cups sitting next to the coffee pot. "You expecting more amigos?"

"No, just you." Ocher says as he takes off his bandana, soaks it with water from the canteen and starts to clean the blood from the injured man's face.

"Amigo, I think he probably needs a doctor."

Ocher rings out the bandana and pours more water on the cloth. "Yep. Do you know if there's one in Fort Stockton?"

"Si, a pretty good one I think."

"I don't think he can ride that far. Best fix up a travois." Ocher continues the clean the wounds.

"Si, I will rig the travois."

"My sister, help sister," chokes the man on the ground. "The note, help my sister. Take my boots."

"All right mister, we'll help your sister. You got a name?"

"Shamus Donnelly. I ain't important. Help my sister. Read the note. The boots."

Ocher starts to respond but can see that the effort has taxed Shamus and he's passed out.

"Senor Ocher, we will help?"

"Baja, there's a saying I recently heard. *In for a penny in for a pound.* Seems to me you bought in, twice. You followed me and then you dealt yourself in when those fellas dropped by. You backing out now?"

"We must discuss how you knew I was following. The other, I am always ready for an adventure, especially one with a caballero like yourself."

Ocher watches Baja fashion the travois noting the ease with which the man works with the rope.

"You've worked as a cowhand, haven't you?" Ocher asks as he continues to clean Shamus's wounds.

"I have been a charro among many other things. Some good, some not so good." Baja responds, picking up the long arms of the travois and walking them over to Shamus's horse.

"You riding in with me?" Ocher asks just as the sun starts to highlight the beauty of the starkness of the desert.

"Senor Ocher, I will wait for you over the ridge just north of here. There is a spring there. It is possible that I may not be welcome in this place. No need to mention that I may have assisted you."

"Ok, Baja. Amigo means friend, doesn't it?"

"Si."

"I'll get Shamus taken care of then join you. We can then share those peaches, amigo."

Chapter Ten

Ocher rides into Fort Stockton. He remembers seeing the sheriff's office during his first ride through so he heads there now.

A short, stocky man's standing just to the left of the door, coffee in hand, a badge pinned to his blue denim shirt. "Had some trouble?"

"Nope. Looking for a doctor. Got one?"

"Yep, step down. I'll send someone to fetch him." He turns toward the open door, "Jubal, go fetch the doc. See that he hurries."

A red-haired young boy, maybe ten or eleven, dragging a broom, steps out. "Yes, Pa," he answers as he races up the dirt street.

"Want to tell me about that one?" the sheriff asks, looking down at Shamus as if he was some kind of carrion.

"Came riding into my camp last night pretty much like you see him. I came through here yesterday and figured this might be the only place that might have a doctor. Cleaned him up a bit. Says his name is Shamus Donnelly.

"Don't know the name. You, I saw yesterday. Braced that cowhand in front of the store.

Trouble seems to settle on you, don't it? Don't need another drifter. Best you turn Shamus there over to the doc and ride on."

Ocher doesn't want to kick up any dust. "Ok, sheriff. As soon as I'm satisfied that Shamus gets taken care of. Not before. Then I'll ride out."

Ocher thinks, *Odd there isn't anybody about. Even this early, there's no one on the street.* He turns as he hears someone coming up the street. Jubal is running with a slim, white-haired man hobbling behind him, trying unsuccessfully to keep up.

The old man looks at the man on the travois then over to Ocher, leans down and checks for a pulse at the side of the beaten man's neck. "Strong pulse, took a whipping. Let's get him over to the office."

Following the doctor, Ocher leads the horse with the travois. The Pinto, sheriff and Jubal are close behind. The sheriff continues to show no interest, still holding his coffee cup.

The doctor and Ocher manage to get the unconscious Shamus through the door and onto a bed. Jubal stays behind to manage the horses.

The doctor pours what smells like alcohol into a blue porcelain basin and starts to clean the wounds.

Shamus moans but remains unconscious.

"What do you know about this, Aaron?" The doctor asks, turning toward the sheriff.

"This fella," pointing toward Ocher, "rode in with that one, said he came into his camp like that."

"Rode in?" The doctor turns toward Ocher, looking at Ocher's hands.

"Yep. Fell off the horse. Came around just a bit and said his name is Shamus Donnelly. Did what I could but figured he needed more care than I could give. Brought him here." Ocher hesitates before continuing. "It wasn't me that did that. I saw you looking at my hands. I'd never have bothered bringing him here if I had."

The doctor smiles and nods his head, "I apologize, but I see too much of this. Someone should be held accountable, especially for this." The doctor glares at the sheriff, "Shamus here didn't get a lick in. Look at his hands. I'd guess he was held while being beaten. Ain't right. He'll recover in time at least from the beating."

"Doc, see that he gets back on his feet," Ocher reaches into his pocket and hands the doctor a ten dollar gold coin. Ocher turns and walks out the door thinking. *This ain't the first beating and that sheriff knows who did this.* "Thanks for watching my horse Jubal," Ocher hands the boy a nickel.

"Thanks, Mister."

Chapter Eleven

Baja's waiting north of Ft Stockton so Ocher heads south. He doesn't trust the sheriff and doesn't want to lead him to Baja or give away his own intentions. He rides south then west, circling the town. After two hours of setting a false trail, Ocher's right back to where Baja left him. He heads north.

"You are a cautious man, amigo. I watch. No one follows," Baja says from the shade of a cedar tree. "But still you come straight to me. You are not as you appear hombre."

"I think the same can be said about you, hombre. I also see that someone else came here." Ocher points to the hoof prints on the ground.

"Si. I think maybe those men will go and find that man Shamus. I send someone to hide him as soon as he can travel."

"Can you cook as well as you can track, Ocher?" Baja asks as they set up camp."

"If I say yes, then I'll end up doing the cooking. If I say no, you'll make the food so bad I'll end up cooking anyway."

"You are indeed a wise man. We will share the cooking. I am a patient man, amigo, but what does the note say?"

Ocher reaches into his pocket, retrieving the note, unfolds it and reads:

Hanna Donnelly, my sister, is being held in servitude in St. Louis, Missouri by a man, Claude Finley. $5000.00 is required to dissolve the debt.

"This man, Shamus, knew he was in trouble. This is the note of a desperate man," Baja says, looking over Ocher's shoulder at the note.

"What is servitude, Baja? Do you know?"

"Si," Baja spits on the ground. "This man Finley paid for, I am guessing, Shamus and Hanna to come to this country. They must work out their debt in some manner before being free."

Ocher looks at the note again, "Indentured servant is another term, Baja, but the same."

"I do not know your word, amigo, but slaves are slaves, no matter the words."

Ocher turns the note over, looks at the back and reverses the note once again. "Where's the money?"

Baja turns over the frying bacon in the skillet. "The boots. Look at the boots."

Ocher smiles, "He did mention the boots more than once." He walks over to Baja's saddle bags and retrieves the boots. He reaches into each boot thinking that Shamus stuffed a map into the toe of one of them. Five thousand dollars certainly won't fit in here.

"Twist the heel, my friend. It is an old trick."

Ocher twists each heel and one by one they come off. In a small cavity in each heel is one half of a map. After placing the two halves together Ocher walks over to Baja. "Make any sense to you?"

Baja places the bacon onto a plate, removes the skillet and takes the map. He studies the document, turns it, cocks his head and finally, "I know this place. It is not far from here."

Ocher takes a piece of the bacon and places it in one of the biscuits Stacey included in his poke. Ocher sees the folded bandana at the bottom of the poke. He reaches in and unfolds it, tying it around his neck. The original bandana left on the wounds of Shamus. "Something on your mind, Baja?"

"Si. Five thousand dollars is a lot of money."

"Yep," Ocher says taking a bite of his biscuit.

"Perhaps I shoot you and just take the money."

"You could try, Baja."

Baja smiles and as he makes his own biscuit, "I would much rather have you as mi amigo. I have enough enemies. We will do this together, if you wish."

"That is what I wish. Besides, I would hate to lose such a good cook," Ocher replies. "Now, that's settled. Have you ever been to St. Louis? What's the best and quickest way to get there?" Ocher asks, taking the next to last biscuit from the bandana.

Baja points toward the bandana, "What's her name, amigo?"

Before Ocher can stop himself, "Stacey."

"The senorita must think much of you. Biscuits and lavender. The last biscuit, would you share that with this poor starving bandito?"

The revelation that biscuits and lavender may have some meaning other than food has never occurred to Ocher, "What do you mean by that?"

"Amigo, there is much in this world I do not understand, especially women. But it is an old custom for a woman to give a scarf or bandana to her man."

Ocher knows Stacey is many miles away but her presence is here. Ocher can't breathe. He begins to sweat and fidget. "Are you sure?"

"There is a simple answer. Return to her wearing the bandana."

"Can we talk about something else?" Ocher stands to retrieve his bedroom.

"Ah hah, the caballero that faced down three men is afraid of this senorita." Baja says as he leans back against the log they had dragged into camp.

"No. Yes. Both."

"It would appear we have something to discuss on our journey."

"Maybe. The journey, how....?"

"There are several choices amigo. Ride north to the rail line and take a train to St. Louis. Go east to Natchez and take a riverboat or railroad. No matter, the journey will take several weeks."

"Which way is the safest?"

"Going north we will be following the routes that the cattle herds are taking. We will encounter some of the night camps. Cowboys are rough but mostly trustworthy." Baja stands, removes his sombrero. Then he moves the coffee pot from the edge of the fire always keeping his gun hand free.

"Is there another way?"

"A river boat. That is a different breed. Gamblers, carpetbaggers, none of them to be trusted. Not so safe."

"All right, Baja, sounds like north. Are there towns to get supplies? Towns where you are welcome?"

"A few," Baja shrugs his shoulders. "The money, amigo. We will get the money first?"

"No, Baja. It's safe where it is. Hanna first, then maybe the money."

"I don't think you trust me, Senor Ocher."

"If I didn't trust you, I would be going alone."

Ocher takes his ground cloth out of his bed roll and spreads it out just outside of the firelight given off by the camp fire. He starts to remove the bandana. Instead inhales the fragrance leaving the bandana in place. *Scariest thing I've done since I got here. Lewis is quite capable of protecting the ranch, but how about Stacey? They got this far without my help.....*

Chapter Twelve

The desert changes slowly from stark waterless sand to rolling hills. Trees appear more and more frequently until they become a common sight. Fresh, clean water also becomes more frequent. The cattle camps are easy to find: just follow the path the cattle have plowed and what they've left behind.

"Hello in the camp," Ocher announces the pairs' presence to the men around the camp fire. Over the last two-plus weeks, Ocher or Baja has made the same call many times.

"Come on in if you're friendly," comes the return.

Ocher and Baja enter the firelight just far enough so that the trail boss can make a decision. They do not step down.

A man needing a shave and, from the dust on his clothes, a bath, pushes back his cowboy hat and inspects the pair. "There's coffee on. Supper will be in a bit if you want. The boys call me Mr. Percy. I'm the trail boss."

"Appreciate the offer. I'm Ocher Jones and this here is..."

"I know who he is. I got no quarrel with you, Baja. Let's keep it that way."

"Senor Percy, I am just a poor vaquero out for a ride with my amigo. There will be no trouble."

"Vittles is on," comes the call from the chuck wagon.

"Let me guess, beans and cornbread," some cowhand retorts.

"This ain't the Delmonico. If you mangy critters can do better, I'll leave you to it," shouts the same voice that had made the chow announcement.

Mr. Percy shakes his head and ambles toward the chuck wagon, "Been a long trip with a lot of beans and cornbread. The boys are getting a mite peevish. We'll be at the rail head in a week. Then they can get paid and eat what they want. Suspect it'll be more drinking than eating. You two headed to the rails?"

"Si. Going to see the elephant," Baja says.

"Ain't heard that in a while," Mr. Percy says as the cook unceremoniously dispenses beans onto the porcelain plate, followed by a huge slice of cornbread.

Ocher doesn't understand the comment but stays silent and tries not to get splattered with the beans launched at his plate. "Thanks."

The cook, startled by the comment, answers "Sure."

Even with so much grumbling about the beans and cornbread, the plates being dumped into the wash bucket are clean of leftovers and no one scrapes any food into the fire, including Ocher's and Baja's.

In one or two of the camps the pair stopped at, after supper there had been some campfire stories and a bit of singing, but not here. Exhausted and full, the hands crawl into their bedrolls to get some sleep before their time to ride night herd. Ocher and Baja turn in as well.

"Don't know if I like the noise of the cattle mulling around or the solitude," Ocher comments to Baja as he spreads out his bedroll.

"As long as the cattle remain calm it is pleasant," Baja responds. "That is why the men sing to them during the night. Although some of the singing is not that pleasant, the cows don't seem to mind."

The sunrise is a long way off when Ocher and Baja grab a biscuit with bacon and hit the trail.

Mr. Percy watches the pair ride out into the darkness and turns toward the cook, "Sure glad the boys didn't try to brace those hombres. I know that Baja is dangerous, but it's the other one I'd stay shy of. He strikes me as a man to leave alone."

The cook hands Mr. Percy a biscuit. "Reminds me of a cougar the way he walks, and his eyes. He don't miss much. Don't wear a gun neither."

Chapter Thirteen

The pair don't generally ride together, making conversation impractical. At night they cook and sleep. During the day they hopscotch, one scouting ahead, the other watching their back trail, as they move north by northeast.

Several long days, after they had shared Mr. Percy's cow camp, Baja says, "Senor, I have been on the trail with you for many days now. You say very little but I learn much just watching. You do not intend to pay this man Finley for the girl, Hanna's release?"

"Don't plan on it."

"That is a good thing. But, we may have to escape those back there and those who will follow from St. Louis."

Ocher nods in agreement, "You have a plan?"

"Si. East of the big town of Wichita, Kansas, about one hundred miles, is a place for water and wood. It is called Nellie's. We will go straight north from here and leave the horses. If we are followed from St. Louis, it would be better to leave the train early. Then disappear into the Oklahoma Territory instead of going all the way into Wichita."

"Nellie's it is," Ocher replies. Before he can ask Baja about Mr. Percy's comment about 'seeing the elephant,' Baja rides off to take point.

Chapter Fourteen

Days, miles, too many early mornings and several cow camps later, "Senor Ocher, we must rest the horses, not to mention my behind. There is a quiet place just ahead. Water and feed for the horses and maybe a fish or two for this poor vaquero."

"Truth be told, Baja, I was ready to rest a couple of days ago. Didn't want you thinking bad of me though. Fresh fish sounds good."

Over fresh fish and pan bread that night, Ocher asks, "Baja, how much further to Nellie's?"

"We are in the Oklahoma Territory. Nellie's is just three or four more days if the weather holds. There are several creeks to cross. If we get rain they will swell and we cannot cross."

"Any Indian troubles this far east?"

"Not Indians..."

The Pinto's ears come up. Ocher looks toward the horse then back to Baja. But Baja has disappeared.

There's no hail from the riders. The four just ride into camp. A thin-faced man with sideburns and several days of beard pushes back his hat, "Where's your friend? I see two saddles." He steps down, without invitation, and starts to walk toward Ocher.

Ocher stands to face the approaching man.

"Evening, Frank," Baja says from just outside the light of fire.

"Baja, that you?"

"Si."

"Little far north for you, ain't it?"

"Perhaps."

Frank takes another step toward Ocher.

"Who's this pilgrim with you?"

Baja steps into the camp.

Frank looks over at Baja then back at Ocher. Frank takes a half step back after looking into the cold darkness of Ocher's eyes.

Baja laughs, "You have just met mi amigo, face to face. As you can plainly see, he is no pilgrim."

One of the riders leans forward in his stirrups and rises up, "Frank, you may want to make peace with that hombre. He's got no gun, but I got a feelin' he don't need one."

The air in the camp's very still. The fire seems silent and the horses aren't moving around.

"Take your brother's advice, Frank. My guess is you are just ahead of a posse anyway," Baja says, standing perfectly still, his hand just above his pistol.

Frank can't hold Ocher's stare any longer, "Next time, mister." He turns and quickly pivots back drawing his gun. The move is supposed to intimidate and surprise Ocher. As Frank finishes the turn, he realizes that he no longer has a gun. Ocher has it.

Ocher stands, still holding the gun at his side by the barrel. "It's settled."

Frank looks back into the eyes of Ocher. "Yes, sir, Mister, I do apologize. There'll be no next time."

Ocher looks at Frank and brushes past him then walks to the man standing up in his stirrups. Ocher hands up the Winchester, "Nice gun, if you need one."

"And have the sense when to use it. I'm Jesse. Thanks for not killing my brother." He accepts the offered pistol. "You're right, Baja. The posse will be along in an hour or two. Let's go, Frank."

"They seem to know you, Baja," Ocher comments after the dust settles from the departing riders.

"Met them down in Mexico a while back. Never rode with them. That is Jesse and Frank James. Do not know the other two. Wanted men around this territory."

"None too friendly either."

"No, Ocher, they are not."

"Do we stay and wait for the posse or ride out, Baja?"

"The horses need to rest and I am not a known man by the law in these parts. We will wait and have coffee ready when they arrive.

The horses don't need to alert the pair in camp that riders are coming. The sound of that many horses makes its own announcement.

Just outside the camp a voice can be heard, "You men go that way. You go that way. No one in or out. Dead or alive men, dead or alive."

Three men ride in. A big man wearing a denim vest and a great big badge, roars, "Some men rode into this camp. How long ago?"

Ocher looks at the man with the badge, "'Bout two hours ago."

"Which way did they go?"

Ocher points due west. "Got some coffee if you want."

The man with the badge takes a long, hard look at Ocher and Baja. "You know who those men are?"

"I do not," Ocher answers, "One called one Frank, and Frank replied to the other one as Jesse. The other two didn't say anything."

The law man pulls a pocket watch, looks at it in the fire light, "Coffee would be good but those boys have to be run down. Best you two ride on out of here first light. Don't like folks I don't know." He turns his horse due west, "Let's go, boys."

Baja looks at Ocher, "Senor. You told him only what he already knew. Telling him otherwise would have been a big mistake."

"Yep. Let's get some rest. Best be out of here by first light."

"Si, amigo."

Chapter Fifteen

The weather cooperates. Ocher and Baja ride into the train stop Nellie's. Just east of a covered platform is a water tank and cords of wood. The rest of the train stop can be seen without standing in the stirrups. A house, store, café and bar all in the same building. The best looking structure in the whole place is the stable. The pair rides there.

A rail thin man, bent over and crippled by age or occupation, steps out of the shade. "Afternoon, gents. Help you?"

"When's the next train headed toward St. Louis?" Ocher asks without stepping down.

"That would be the four o'clock train. Should be here by six, maybe."

"We might be gone a week or more. Take care of the horses that long?" Baja asks.

"Sure mister, happens all the time. Have to get some money up front. Feed ain't cheap."

Ocher steps down, "The Pinto ain't quite housebroke yet. Best be careful. He might fuss a bit."

"Some say the same about me. We'll get along just fine," the man says taking the reins of both horses. "The old woman's up at the house, got something cooking. Take your chances. Pay her. You pay me, well... I'd probably sneak off and gamble it away. Just pay her."

On the way to the house Ocher can hear the sound of chickens. He looks over at Baja. "Fried chicken sounds good."

"Si, anything's better than what we cook."

The store/café/bar is one room. Two long tables bracket the bar with several half-filled shelves at the back. It smells good though.

"Howdy," comes from a grizzled old woman with clear blue eyes that sparkle with mischief. "Got some chicken and biscuits ready and a peach pie coming out soon. Interested?"

"Si, senorita," Baja responds.

"No need for flattery. Ain't been a senorita for a while. Appreciate the gesture anyway. Sit, it'll be right out. Milk, tea or coffee?"

"Milk," both men respond.

At around five o'clock waiting for the four o'clock train, "Don't believe I could eat another piece of that pie. Might give it a try though," Ocher says rubbing his stomach.

"Si."

"I've never been on a train before. Have you, Baja?"

"I have never ridden on one before, but I have been in them."

Ocher ponders the meaning of the statement finally, "You've robbed a train?"

"Maybe, but my family needed the money."

Ocher accepts the train part but, "We've been on the trail together for a while. You never speak of your family."

"I could say the same about you, amigo."

Ocher stretches his legs out. "I have no family, haven't since I was eight."

"That is triste. How you say in English? Sad. A man must have family to be a man. You met my family."

"The old man and girl in Ft. Stockton?"

"Si. I was riding after you to thank you for defending my sister when we became amigos."

"That's all that's left of your family?"

"Blood family. Si. You don't have to be kin to be a family. I think maybe the senorita, whose scarf you wear, could become family."

Ocher doesn't know how to respond, "I have met many kind and generous people since I came here. Maybe they think of me as family."

Chapter Sixteen

The serenity of the evening changes just as gradually as the sound of the approaching train noises intrude on the mood. It starts with the railroad tracks vibrating, followed by the bellowing of the train as it assaults the station.

"Senor Ocher, amigo, we should not travel together. It could be inconvenient for you if I must leave quickly. There may be some who recognize me from other trains. In St. Louis there is a place on the waterfront, The Barge. A friend, Peso, works as a... I have no word... a peon for the owner. Peso has only four fingers on his left hand. He is a trusted friend. This place, The Barge, is not a pleasant place. Be careful."

"You be careful, amigo."

Baja strolls toward the front of the train as Ocher stands and walks toward the back. Ocher steps up into one of the passenger cars and finds a seat in the last row. Before taking his seat next to the window, he surveys the rest of the car. There are three men and two women sharing the car. Ocher senses nothing that concerns him.

He settles in, places his saddle bags on the aisle seat, stretches out his legs, then pulls his hat down over his eyes. He's startled when the train's engine struggles against the weight of the attached passenger and freight cars, trying to gain momentum. He's seen the terrain, and, by the time the landscape might change, it'll be too dark to see, so he goes back to resting.

Over the next two and a half days Ocher moves through the passenger cars, just for the exercise, sees Baja, but doesn't acknowledge him. At several of the depot stops, he steps off the train and purchases food, water and a newspaper. There's no mention of Claude Finley in the papers. The landscape does change but for the most part its rolling hills. One hill's much like the rest. His enjoyment and anticipation of the train ride has long since waned. *I'll be glad to get off this beast and back in the saddle. I wonder what Stacey is doing? Is she safe? Boyd wouldn't dare hurt the women.*

It's midnight when Ocher steps off the train. Over the last full day the car, he's been riding in, fills up. He has to give up the seat next to him and put his saddlebags in a basket looking thing above his seat.

The crush of people is amazing. San Francisco had, at least up to now, what he considered a lot of people. There are a lot more here. Draping his saddlebags over his shoulder, Ocher walks as quickly as possible away from the depot.

The smell of fresh baked goods draws his attention to a small bakery shop. "Apple pie smells good and some milk to go with it, please."

In a conversation with the baker, Ocher learns that the cheap hotels are around the river front. The more comfortable ones are several blocks away. They cost a little more but are a bit safer. After finishing his pie, Ocher walks the half mile to the recommended High Plains Hotel.

The clerk eyes Ocher up and down, turns the register toward him, "That'll be two dollars per night, in advance. How long you intend to stay?"

"I'll let you know when it's convenient," Ocher says, flipping a five-dollar gold piece that lands on the desk."

The clerk looks at the coin and then at Ocher, finally smiling. "We have a bath house next door and a tailor available if you require."

"I think I probably need both. A bath for sure." Ocher takes the key and starts up the stairs noting that the floor at his end of the hall squeaks. *Good to know.*

At first light, Ocher enters the bath house. The attendant is also the barber. Ocher takes advantage of both. As he emerges from the bath area into the changing room, a man dressed in a suit, glasses, full beard, with big white teeth showing through the beard, is standing. "Good morning, Mr. Jones, I am Argost the tailor. The hotel clerk, Mr. Stiles, sent word that you may need my services."

"Word gets around pretty quick, but yes, I do need something to wear to call on a local gentleman."

"May I inquire as to whom you are meeting? That could make your choice much easier."

Ocher decides to tell the tailor, if nothing else, just to judge his reaction, "Mr. Claude Finley."

Mr. Argost can't stifle his reaction. He inhales a large breath, exhales slowly and looks at Ocher, "Finley a friend of yours?"

"No. I know very little about him."

Mr. Argost smiles, "Something that would protect your back might be appropriate."

"I am familiar with that sort. Does he have friends in the community?"

"Mr. Jones, I have said too much already..."

"Mr. Argost, I do know he's holding a young woman in servitude and I intend to take her to her brother. Anything you can tell me would be helpful."

"Mr. Jones, he has many a young woman in servitude. If they can't pay back his fees in what he considers an appropriate length of time, he forces the women, especially the younger ones, to work in the bars along the waterfront. Very few escape there as young as they entered. Not in age anyway."

"Thank you, Mr. Argost. That's helpful. My friends do not address me as Mr. Jones. The name is Ocher."

"Please don't laugh but I am Argost Argost. My parents could not read or write. They had 'Argost' written down somewhere and thought it would be easier to spell the only name they knew."

"It just makes it easier for me to remember, Argost. Now, about some clothes. Nothing fancy. I will have further need of your services and it may be on a moment's notice or the middle of the night. Is that a problem?"

"Not if it hurts Finley. I will be at your service anytime. Here's a card. I live above the shop."

"One more thing. Could you make arrangements to have this note delivered to Mr. Finley? It's a request for an appointment."

"No problem."

Ocher decides two things. One: dress in his trail clothes and two: visit The Barge in those clothes. From Baja's description, The Barge is along the river front.

Ocher makes the walk, observing the similarities and differences of St. Louis and San Francisco. As in San Francisco, the closer to the working water front, the less genteel the area becomes. Fancy clothes and gentle manners wane quickly. The Barge typifies the area, rough-hewn exterior, a make-shift red sign hanging askew, and men moving about in various stages of drunkenness. Not much different from the docks of San Francisco.

Ocher enters The Barge and strides to the bar as if he's accustomed to the surroundings. The smoke and raucous talk's overwhelming. "Beer," he yells at the bartender, placing a nickel on the counter. Accepting the beer, he turns to face the room. Seeing a small empty table against one wall, he wades into the crowd and takes command of the table.

A scuffle begins on the far side of the room. The combatants are ushered out the doors by several large men followed by the majority of the occupants.

"Ever been to California?" asks a short Mexican man as he wipes the 'clean' table with his left hand, a hand missing a finger.

"Yes, I have. Never been to the Baja region though," Ocher responds, taking a sip of the beer. "That's awful." He grimaces, setting the mug on the now clean table.

"Si. The cervesa here is dreadful. You should leave and find a better place. You should leave now while they are all outside," Peso says, taking Ocher's beer mug and walking away.

Ocher steps out into the street, turns away from the brawl in progress and heads away from the river front. Two men step away from the contest and fall in behind Ocher. He feels them immediately.

He decides that confronting the men this close to the river front might invite participation from their friends. Better to get them away and into a more private setting. Just as Ocher decides on a location to have a discussion with his followers, Baja steps out of a store front.

"Those are amigos of mine," he says pointing with his chin.

The two men walk across the street and sit down on a rock wall.

"Just in case."

"Thanks. It's good to see you, Baja."

Baja smiles and pulls Ocher into the shadows next to the store. "This man Finley. He is not a nice man. He has friends. To steal this woman will be difficult. Do you have a plan, amigo?"

"I have the start of one. I'll learn more when I visit him in the morning. I have sent a note requesting an appointment."

"Be careful. This man is not to be trusted. You will be watched, my friend. There will always be two men close by if you need them. When you need me, just ask them and I will come."

"Thanks. Be ready. Tomorrow night if all goes well."

"Si."

Ocher steps back onto the sidewalk, and leading the two men, heads to his hotel.

Chapter Seventeen

The evening is quiet. No one approaches his room setting off the squeaking floor. His new clothes arrive and Ocher is dressed and ready for breakfast.

As he enters the lobby, the night clerk says, "Mr. Jones, a note for you."

The note is handwritten:

I will receive you at 10:00 today.
C. Finley

Good, Ocher thinks. *Maybe by this time tomorrow you will regret receiving me.*

After scratching at his new clothes through breakfast, Ocher takes the time to familiarize himself with the surrounding of Mr. Finley's residence. Promptly at ten, Ocher knocks on the large double oak doors. A black man dressed in a well-fitting black suit, white shirt and black tie, opens the door.

"May I help you, sir?"

"I have a ten o'clock appointment with Mr. Finley."

"Yes, sir. Wait here and I will see if he's available."

Ocher has anticipated the tactic of Mr. Finley and waits, what he thinks is a reasonable amount of time, then opens the door and enters.

Ocher can hear Finley's voice, trying to establish the impression of control, from down the hall, "Make him wait five more minutes and then show him in."

"No need, Mr. Finley, I am already in. Ten o'clock means ten o'clock," Ocher states as he enters what appears to be a library.

Claude Finley is a portly man dressed in a well-tailored suit open at the neck. The reason for the open shirt is obvious because his jowls and neck couldn't fit in a buttoned collar. A large cigar is burning in a crystal ash tray.

Mr. Finley picks up the cigar, "Logan that will be all. Send in Hanna with coffee." Claude Finley glares at Ocher through the cigar smoke with small, black, lifeless eyes. "You're rather impertinent," he glances down at the note on his desk. "Mr. Jones."

Ocher does not answer.

"What can I do for you?"

"Coffee first."

A young woman with auburn hair, green eyes and a defeated walk carries a tray to a side table.

"Will that be all, Mr. Finley?"

"Ok, Mr. Jones. There's your coffee. Hanna, pour Mr. Jones a cup."

As Hanna hands Ocher the coffee, he whispers, "Hanna Donnelly?"

Her eyes widen, but, with her back turned to Finley, Finley can't see her expression. She nods slightly.

As Ocher takes the cup, he slips a piece of paper into her hand, "Thank You."

"That will be all, Hanna."

The two men alone, Ocher sets down the coffee. "I've come to pay the debt owed by Hanna Donnelly."

"Ah." Mr. Finley says laying his cigar back in the ash tray. "You have the money?"

"I have what is owed you," Ocher replies not wanting to lie.

"Well, fine. However, since Hanna has been in my employ, she's incurred some additional expenses, clothing, food and some medical needs. The original debt plus these expenses amount to, let me see." Finley opens a drawer on the right side of the desk and pulls out a ledger. "She now owes six thousand, four hundred and fifty-five dollars. Would you like to see the ledger?"

"No, that won't be necessary. Please have Hanna ready this time tomorrow with a signed document stating that she's no longer indebted to you. For anything. After I read the document and am satisfied with Hanna's condition, payment will be made."

"All legal, as it should be. Ten o'clock tomorrow, Mr. Jones. You didn't drink you coffee."

"Would you like to drink it, Mr. Finley?"

Claude Finley smiles, "No, I don't think I would. Tomorrow, payment in full."

Ocher walks to the front door. Logan's holding the door open, "Be wary, sir. Be wary."

Chapter Eighteen

Ocher walks through the front gate of the estate and onto the street. He smiles as he notes that the street around Finley's place is becoming very crowded. Ocher can see the two men who had followed him from the hotel and Baja with Peso. In addition, two rough looking men in suits have arrived from the alley beside Finley's residence. Ocher needs to talk to Baja and doesn't want Finley's men to see the conversation.

Ocher starts toward the river front with Finley's men in tow. Baja signals his people to remain in place. Ocher walks about half a block and reverses course. Now he's walking straight at Finley's men.

"Can I help you, boys?" Ocher asks, stopping just short of the pair.

The bigger of the two, the one with a broken nose, says, "Mr. Finley is providing protection. Us."

"I don't need his protection. Especially from you two."

"What do you mean by that?" Broken nose says taking a tentative step forward.

"You two can't protect yourselves. You certainly can't protect me."

The spokesman steps forward, raising his hands with the intent of pushing Ocher. Instead Ocher steps forward leading with his forehead. The man with the broken nose experiences the same event. Ocher's forehead impacts the man's nose and the blood flows onto the man's shirt. The other gentleman starts to reach under his left arm for a pistol. Ocher reaches back between his shoulder blades and produces his black obsidian knife.

The man with the bloody nose mumbles something through the hand covering his face. The man reaching for his gun turns slightly to listen to what the mumbling man is saying. In that instant Ocher has the point of the knife under the man's chin.

"You need to take care of your friend. If Finley still feels I need protection, I'm staying at the High Plains."

As Ocher walks away he can hear the man with the gun, "What were you trying to say?"

"Watch out. He has a knife."

Ocher continues toward the river. He finds a secluded spot and waits for Baja.

Baja and Peso join Ocher. "Gentlemen, I hope your evening's free. We have plans to make."

Peso smiles, "I like this gringo. He is very entertaining and dangerous."

"Thank you, Peso. Now down to business. Baja, can you have some men watch Finley's so they don't take Hanna out."

"Si.

Ocher spends the next hour explaining the plan. Baja and Peso make a few suggestions formalizing the events. "Peso, it's been a pleasure. Baja, I hope to see you soon. Be careful, amigo."

Baja nods his approval of the plan, "The young lady and I will await you at Nellie's. You be careful. Mi amigos will be there if you need them. Adios."

Ocher returns to his room. At supper time he ventures down to the dining room in the hotel. As he passes through the lobby, he nods to the man with the broken nose. His bloody clothing is replaced and the other man's not in the lobby.

They're probably taking turns watching me, Ocher muses as he enters the dining room.

Chapter Nineteen

The sun is just melting through the windows, dissolving the darkness, when Ocher hears the floor squeak out in the hall. The tell-tale squeak is followed by a hammering on the door. "You, Jones, get up. Mr. Finley wants you. I mean right now."

Ocher opens the door, "Good morning. Mr. Finley wants to see me, does he? Well, I'll be along after breakfast." He closes the door and steps back.

The door disintegrates as the man with the broken nose shoulders his way through the door and into the room. Behind him is the second man, this time holding a gun pointed at Ocher.

"Breakfast can wait, I suppose."

Outside the High Plains a carriage is waiting. The man with the broken nose gets in, dragging Ocher with him. The other man, still aiming the gun at Ocher, follows.

They arrive at Finley's just as the sun makes its full appearance in the east. Ocher's hustled into the library.

"You! You stole my ledger. You kidnapped Hanna," Claude Finley blares through the spittle as he points at Ocher.

Ocher remains silent.

From the library door Logan asks, "Coffee anyone?"

Ocher turns and sees Logan smiling.

"I'd like some coffee, Logan, it it's not too much trouble," Ocher responds to the offer.

"No trouble for you, Mr. Jones. No trouble at all."

"Enough. Where's my journal? Where's Hanna?" Finley screams, his face getting redder.

"I have no idea what you're talking about, Mr. Finley. I was in my room all night. Ask your people," Ocher says pointing toward the two men standing to his left.

Finley continues his tirade when someone bangs on the front door.

"Trouble, Mr. Finley?" the question comes from a large red-headed man standing in the library door. Right behind the man, Peso materializes and smiles at Ocher.

"Shanahan, what are you doing here?" Finley asks, the volume of the question toned down only slightly.

"Heard that there might have been a little trouble here. Law and order, Mr. Finley. That's what I get paid for."

"Arrest that man. He stole my ledger and kidnapped one of my girls," Finley yells pointing at Ocher. "Last night a mob of hooligans broke in here and took my things. I want them back."

"Hooligans, Mr. Finley. Are you implying that some of our fine Irish lads had something to do with this?"

"I don't know, but he had something to do with this," Finley continues accusing Ocher and pointing.

Shanahan turns toward Ocher, pushing back his coat lapel showing a badge. "I'm Sergeant Kacey Shanahan. Who might you be?"

"Ocher Jones, Sergeant."

"Mr. Jones, did you steal Mr. Finley's ledger and kidnap one of his girls?"

"I was in my room all night and didn't leave. Ask those two. Mr. Finley kindly provided me some protection while I'm visiting."

Shanahan looks at the man with the bandage on his nose. "Did Mr. Jones leave his room last night?"

"No, but..."

Peso is now standing next to Logan in the doorway of the library.

"I have no reason to arrest Mr. Jones. But since you are a respected member of our community, I'll require Mr. Jones to leave town immediately."

Mr. Finley collapses in his chair, "He stole all my records and kidnapped Hanna Donnelly and that's all you can do? Make him leave. What do I pay you cops for?"

"Mr. Finley, I'm insulted that I can be bought. That's an outrage. I have never. You are, well you know what you are, with Irish girls especially. You are a disgrace," Shanahan states as he stands in front of the desk, with each statement pushing the desk at Finley.

"Mr. Jones, there's a nine o'clock train leaving for the west. I'll make sure you are on it. Come along." He takes Ocher by the arm and leads him toward the front door.

In the library Finley is screaming threats against the police, the Irish and his two men.

Logan mouths, "Well done," as they pass.

"Just keep walking, Ocher. I'll answer your questions later," Shanahan says as he releases Ocher's arm.

Chapter Twenty

After they reach the privacy of the street, Shanahan looks at Ocher. "Mr. Ocher Jones, I'm not going to ask any questions. I really don't want to know the answers anyway. Claude Finley is not a man. He's been a disease to this community for years. He has, as he said, paid some within the police to protect him. With that ledger gone... well, maybe that will financially cripple him. I hope so. I suspect Hanna's release document was in the ledger, but I don't want to know.

"If I were to come across the ledger would it be of value to the police department, Sergeant?" Ocher asks Shanahan.

"It's Kacey. No. It would probably end up back in his hands. So, no. If you come across it somehow, burn it."

"I'm curious, Kacey. Where does Peso fit in all of this?"

Shanahan looks at Peso and Peso nods.

"Peso can move about in places the cops can't. He hears things. Let's leave it at that."

"Ok. Good to have friends," Ocher smiles at Peso.

"Ocher, I don't intend to stand around and wait for that train. Your friend Peso has made arrangements for your saddlebags. Get a ticket and be gone. Finley won't let this go. It may take him a while but he'll probably take a run at you somehow. Take care." Shanahan turns and walks through the crowd.

Peso guides Ocher to a quiet spot along one wall of the rail station. One of Baja's men hands Ocher his saddlebags. "It has been a pleasure watching you work, Senor Ocher. Say adios to my cousin Baja, if you see him." Peso walks away.

"Peso, do you have the ledger?" Ocher asks.

"Si."

"Good, put it to good use, amigo."

"Si."

Ocher throws his saddlebags over his shoulder and strolls through the crowd toward the ticket booth. He passes a well-dressed Mexican gentleman sporting a brand new tailored coat over a colorful vest and tailored pants. The gentleman is accompanied by his son, also well-dressed in fitted trousers and a loose fitting coat topped off with a cowboy hat. A small sprig of auburn hair sticks out. Ocher winks at Baja as they pass.

Chapter Twenty-One

The two-and-a-half day journey is no different than the two-and-a-half day trip had been the other way. Ocher sees Baja and son several times but stays clear, watching to see if anyone shows interest in him or the other two.

At Nellie's the three get off the train. Baja and son proceed to the store while Ocher watches the activity around the train. Water and lumber are loaded. No one else gets on or off and the train heads out going west. Ocher strolls toward the store.

"Welcome back," the grizzled old woman says. "They've already ordered for you. Sit, it'll be right out."

Ocher walks to the table and sits down next to Hanna. "When can I change out of these clothes, mister?"

"Let's clear the station and then you can change," whispers Ocher. "Don't want these folks to see a boy ride in and a girl ride out. Might spark some interest we don't want."

"All right, and thanks," she responds.

After dinner the three purchase supplies and haggle over the price of another horse and a pack mule. The only time during the transaction that makes the old woman pause is when Baja's son asks for some scented soap.

By sundown the three are miles south of Nellie's and getting more confident about their escape.

The first night's camp is in a small cut-back with a fresh stream, feeding several waterfalls.

Before camp assignments can be determined, Hanna, carrying scented soap and clothes, heads to the pool below the last waterfall. Ocher and Baja set up camp as they've done many times.

"This one is strong willed," Baja says to Ocher as they collect additional wood for the fire. "She will determine how she wants the camp to run."

"Fine by me," Ocher says, piling the wood next to the fire.

Hanna returns, wearing a riding skirt, a blue blouse and a dark blue vest. She carries her old clothes and cowboy hat. Her auburn hair flows down over her shoulders.

"Hanna, nice to see you again," Ocher says pouring beans into a skillet.

"Thank you, Mr. Jones."

"I'm Ocher and that's Baja."

Hanna sits by the fire watching the cooking. She accepts her bacon and beans. After her first bite, "If you two don't mind, I'll take over the cooking the rest of the way."

Both men nod, accepting her offer.

"Baja, I see that you wear a gun. Can you use it?"

"A little bit, senorita."

"Good, I'm sure there must be some wild game around. We can have bacon and beans only so much. Wild game will be better and I'll add some herbs I can pick along the way."

"Si, Senorita Hanna. I will do my best."

"Why did you two come for me and not Shamus?"

Baja looks at Ocher, "He came to your camp. You tell her."

"Shamus was badly beaten and stumbled into my camp and asked for help. He was taken to a doctor. When he arrived at my camp, he gave me a note and begged me to help his sister, Hanna. There isn't much else to tell. We came and got you and now we'll take you to Shamus."

Hanna's quiet for a long time. "Thank you."

Chapter Twenty-Two

As the days go by, Hanna changes in contrast to the terrain. The trees thin out, giving way to the rolling hills, and then the almost lifeless sandy soil. Hanna blooms from the defeated girl who delivered coffee at Finley's, to a radiant and far more confident woman. Certainly not shy.

After four days of dawn to dusk riding, "Gentlemen, you two are accustomed to trail life. I'm not, at least not yet. I'm sore, dirty and tired," Hanna proclaims, her arms folded across her chest. "I'm going down to that deep pool of water and take a bath. But before I do that, I'm going to wash my clothes and put on my boy clothes while my other things dry. I expect you to remain the gentlemen you are. Tomorrow I rest. Any questions?"

Baja smiles, "No, senorita. Maybe one question."

"Yes," Hanna responds, taking out her scented soap and boy clothes.

"Do I have to eat Ocher's cooking tonight?"

Hanna laughs and shakes her head. "No, Baja, when I finish I'll cook supper."

After supper Ocher's out gathering wood and checking the perimeter.

"Are the nights always this magnificent?" Hanna asks, pouring an after-supper coffee for Baja.

"Si, Senorita Hanna," Baja says, accepting his cup.

"Is everybody as nice as you two?"

"It is the same here as it is where you came from. Some good, some not so good. That one," he points to Ocher with his coffee cup in his left hand. "He is an hombre, a man, a friend to have. There are very few like him. That is why I came on this adventure. To watch him."

"I don't understand, Baja. Watch him?"

"Si, senorita. Most men are driven by greed, lust, fear or the need for power. This one," he nods toward Ocher, "he does not seek these things. He is driven by honor, to do the right thing always. I have learned much by just watching."

"Are all cowboys like him?" Hanna asks, now more intrigued than ever.

"He is not a cowboy. I suspect he knows very little of cows. He is a predator against how you say, cosas malvadas. Bad things, evil things. He defended Shamus without knowing anything about your brother. He was not afraid of the men who rode into his camp. He even knew that I was out in the darkness. How he knows these things is a mystery to a poor bandito like myself."

Ocher returns to camp, drops the wood and accepts a coffee from Hanna. He's surprised when she kisses him on the cheek as she says, "Thank you."

The ride south through the Oklahoma Territory and into Texas is without incident. Baja and Ocher agree that avoiding the cattle drive camps is prudent. A young, auburn haired woman would certainly be the talk of the trails.

The cattle herds are easy to avoid. The noise of thousands of cattle complaining, the dust and the cowboys caterwauling at the herd announce their presence well in advance.

Just after dusk one evening Baja walks back into camp with an arm load of wood. "Senor Ocher, I do not understand."

"What don't you understand, Baja?" Ocher replies.

"This woman, she shows no interest in me. Amigo, that is strange. All women love Baja."

"She probably does love you, my friend. She just has no need of you."

"I do not understand."

"If I'm right, you'll see very soon. You say maybe five or six days to your grandfather's place?"

"Si. We will arrive midday. There is a place we will wait and watch the hacienda. After dark we will go down."

Hanna returns to the camp from the spring, carrying a full canteen over her shoulder and two hands full of reddish clay. She plops the clay down next to the three prairie grouse that Ocher killed with his stone sling. Hanna reaches for the first bird and starts to pack the fowl into the clay.

"Aren't you gonna pluck those first?" Ocher asks.

"No need. You boys cleaned them. Now all I have to do is stuff them with some greens, wrap them in some of this red clay and bake them. Just like we used to do with pheasants. When they are done all you have to do is break open the clay and the feathers will come right off." Hanna responds, as she picks up some vegetation she gathered and pushes into the bird. She covers the three prairie grouse in clay, places them in a small depression next to the fire. She rakes dirt over the clay balls and then covers the dirt with coals from the fire. "The birds will be ready in about an hour. I'm going to gather some more greens from around the marsh."

Baja shakes his head, "This woman and her greens. If only she could find some peppers. I must not complain too much. Her cooking is far better than ours. I really don't miss the bacon and beans."

"Far better than the tasteless rice and chicken that I was raised on," Ocher replies, watching Hanna disappear around a copse of cattail.

On her return, Hanna rolls the clay balls from the fire using a stick. "Let them cool a bit then break it open and the feathers will stick to the clay. The bird will be ready to eat. There's some more cooked greens as well. I expect you to eat both."

Baja and Ocher don't argue with Hanna. They learned early on, the more they complain the worse the food becomes, if they get anything at all. They choke down the greens and then devour the birds. Even the coffee is better.

Ocher and Baja scour their plates with sand and present their clean plates to Hanna for inspection. "I'll just rinse them off a bit," she says as she does every evening. "Are we getting close?"

"Si, senorita. In fact we are close to the place where mi amigo met Shamus. Perhaps it is time we help the horses keep watch."

"Really, Baja. You think those men might be out prowling about?" Hanna asks as she packs the plates in a saddle bag.

Ocher smiles, "I see you're learning the ways of the trail. You packed everything in camp, just in case we have to leave in a hurry. We'll keep watch. Just in case. You want first or second watch, Baja?"

"I will take first watch."

"You two have been so kind I hate to ask this, but did you mention some buried money?" Hanna asks.

"I did not wish to offend you, my good friend. When are we going to get the money?" Baja adds.

"We aren't. As soon as we reunite Hanna with Shamus, and I rest the Pinto, I'm heading to Mexico to meet a Senor Tyler Gomez. I trust you to take Hanna and Shamus to their money."

"Senor Ocher, that is a lot of trust to place on a bandito as myself." He pauses, changing the position of his outstretched legs. "It will be so. You have bought me a fine set of new clothes so I will do as you ask. You do not wish that I go with you to the Patron Gomez?"

"Am I safe alone?"

"Si, I will send word. You will not be bothered."

Three days later the troop arrives at a mesa overlooking a small valley. Baja leads them to a shaded overhang that has a small tank of water at the back. He points out toward the valley. "That is my grandfather's ranch. It is small but it is all he can manage by himself. We will wait here until dark. No fire, Senorita Hanna." Baja walks to the edge of the mesa and stands looking at the ranch. "I believe the ranch is not being watched."

"How do you know that?" Hanna asks.

"See the corrals at the back of the main house?"

"Yes".

"The corrals are east and west of the casa. There are no horses in those corrals. If there was someone watching, there would be horses in one of those corrals. There is no place to watch the ranch in the north or south, only east and west. My abuelo would place a horse for each person watching in the appropriate corral. There are no horses."

Hanna looks at Baja, "Now why would you be so cautious?"

Baja just smiles, "One can never tell, senorita."

Baja leads the riders down the mesa to the ranch. Two men appear at the door. As they approach the front of the adobe building, the man with the lamp steps out onto the porch. Ocher recognizes the man as the old man sitting in the wagon in Ft. Stockton. The other man is Shamus.

Hanna leaps from her horse and runs into the arms of Shamus. The embrace is followed by a kiss. Not a kiss a brother would give a sister.

Baja looks over at Ocher, "I do not understand amigo."

"Shamus is Hanna's husband, not her brother."

Baja looks at the pair and back at Ocher, "How did you know?"

"She never, not once, referred to Shamus as her brother."

"But..."

"He said she was his sister. She never said brother."

Baja laughs a big raucous laugh, "She has no need of Baja. Amigo, I think maybe we should sleep in the barn tonight. The horses will be much more quiet."

Before Ocher can respond, a tornado of long black hair in a flowered dress leaps into Baja's arms.

"Did you bring me anything, hermano?" she asks.

"I brought you him," Baja says pointing at Ocher. "But he is taken, I think. That bandana once smelled of lavender. And the other lady, she can cook."

"I can cook and I don't need your help, Baja. Put me down."

"No, little one, you are right. You do not need my help. You are turning into a beautiful desert flower." Baja lowers the young girl to the ground. "This is my lovely and almost grown up sister, Corina."

Corina tries to kick Baja, but he just steps back.

"Corina, these are my friends. Ocher and that one is Hanna."

Shamus walks over to Ocher and Baja. Hanna is holding his hand. "I can't thank you enough." Hanna pulls at his hand toward the house.

"We can talk later," Ocher says.

Chapter Twenty-Three

"Good morning, gentlemen," Hanna says as she enters the barn carrying coffee to Ocher and Baja. "And thank you, again."

"And how was your evening with your brother?" Baja teases.

"You be quiet," Hanna says, kicking hay at Baja. "And I'll be hearing nothing from you either, Ocher Jones."

"The coffee is as good as ever." Ocher smiles.

"Breakfast will be ready when you get to the house," she says as she turns. "Not one word."

Corina is busy setting plates full of food on the table when Baja and Ocher walk into the kitchen.

Baja walks to the head of the table where Thomas, the grandfather, is sipping coffee. "It is good to see you, abuelo. You are looking well."

The old man just nods at Baja and looks at Ocher. "You are welcome here always. It is humble but safe."

"Thank you, sir," Ocher replies, sensing that is an appropriate response.

"Hermanita, little sister, be kind to my amigo with your cooking. He has not had the pleasure of your spices and peppers," Baja says as he passes Corina and kisses her on the top of her head.

"I think maybe it's too late," Corina says pointing at the table.

Ocher's face is blood red, sweat pouring down his face as he gasps for air.

Shamus is laughing as he hands a glass of milk to Ocher. "I'm still not used to those peppers. Once you can breathe they aren't bad. This is breakfast, wait 'til supper. They get hotter."

Thomas says nothing, just keeps eating the peppers having little or no effect on him.

After Corina serves the food, she sits across from Hanna and Shamus.

"Amigo, are you still going into Mexico to see Tyler Gomez?" Baja asks as he takes a second portion of scrambled egg and peppers.

"Yes. I want to get supplies and let the Pinto rest a day or so. If I can survive Corina's cooking I'll leave in a couple of days."

Shamus leans forward and hesitantly asks Ocher, "Did Finley try to charge you more than we owed?"

"Funny thing about that... let's just say the money is still where you left it. Baja will take you safely to it. After that, it's a big country."

"We'll have to think on that now. With that money things might be a bit easier. Depends. Can't thank you enough."

"I got to go and see the big city of St. Louis. Didn't get to see the elephant. Maybe next time."

"See the elephant?" Shamus asks.

"Baja explained it to me," Ocher says in between gulps of milk. "Years ago it meant seeing military action for the first time. Now it means going to the big city where the action is."

"And the painted ladies for the first time," Thomas adds.

"Baja didn't mention that part," Ocher says looking at Baja.

Baja just shrugs his shoulders.

Ocher eats just enough to satisfy his hunger, the hot peppers curbing his appetite.

Corina glances at Ocher's plate, "You did not eat so much, Ocher. I will not be so generous with the peppers next time."

"That will hold me for a while. At least 'til I get back from picking up supplies."

"Ocher, mi hijo, my son, the sheriff in town would not welcome you. There are a few supplies that we need. Perhaps it would be better if Corina and I go and get what you need," Thomas offers.

"I will go far enough to watch and not be seen. I don't wish the sheriff to make you feel unwelcome," Ocher says after taking another drink of milk.

"I will go as well, abuelo," Baja says, taking a third helping of breakfast.

Over the next four days, Ocher, Baja and Shamus, under the supervision of Thomas, repair or replace things that Thomas wants repaired or replaced. Somehow Hanna convinces Corina to share cooking duties. Ocher eats some of Corina's cooking and a lot of Hanna's. The Pinto stands in the shade.

The day dawns with Ocher in the saddle ready for the trip south. After handshakes, hugs, and a *via con dios* from Thomas, Ocher rides out of the yard and heads toward Mexico.

The ride takes six days. Days in which Ocher enjoys the solitude and at the same time misses the companionship of friends and the scent of lavender. The leisurely ride through rain, mud, dust, wind, and hot coffee is tolerable. Thankfully, Hanna prevailed in packing Ocher's grub bag. Milk, to tame the fiery peppers, is mighty hard to find out on the trail. Hanna's food lasts only five of the six days. The last night, Ocher endures his own bland cooking.

Ocher holds up about half-a-mile from the ranch allowing ranch hands to observe him. He sees little or no activity. The Pinto doesn't seem nervous so Ocher rides on toward the ranch.

The Gomez Hacienda is located upstream of the small village of Sabinos. The town and the church were built after the land grant was proclaimed to the Gomez family. The adobe buildings used as living areas are arranged in a semi circle with the livestock buildings also downstream on the Sabinos River. The entrance to the hacienda is through a large covered arch into a courtyard adorned with plants and trees.

Ocher rides through the archway, stopping at a respectable distance, and stays in the saddle. He knows not to step down until invited. A man of undeterminable age with braids showing from under a wide brim sombrero walks up to the rider and Pinto.

After an appraisal of the pair, he says. "Buenos Dias, senor, how may I help you?"

"Buenos Dias, I have come to see the Patron. Here is a letter of introduction from Senor Livingston." Ocher hands the man a letter taken from his pocket.

"Please step down. There is water for you and your horse." He points toward a water trough situated under a large Eucalyptus tree. There are several gourds hanging from the lower branches, the cool water causing the gourds to sweat.

Ocher walks the Pinto to the trough and allows him to take a quick drink. Only after the Pinto is cool to the touch does he let him loose to enjoy a long drink. After attending to the Pinto, Ocher dips a cool drink for himself. As he takes a second dipper full, the Patron steps into the shade.

Tyler Gomez would appear to be a simple vaquero except that his clothes are tailor made. His stride and posture tell you his position. He doesn't overwhelm but there's no mistake about his being the Patron. Ocher notes that the letter is in his left hand and hasn't been opened.

"Welcome, senor, to our hacienda. It is late. Please stay the night and take advantage of our hospitality. I am Tyler Gomez, your humble servant." He holds out his hand.

Ocher takes the offered hand. "I am Ocher Jones. It would be my pleasure to stay the night."

Gomez smiles, turns to the pig-tailed man. "Manny, please take care of Senor Jones' horse, we will be in the arbor."

Tyler Gomez takes almost a minute before he speaks. "Come join us for supper. Then, get some rest. We can speak later about why you have come here."

Ocher has shared the table with the chaos of Ollie's house, the terror of sitting across from Stacey and cow camps. The Gomez gathering is quite different. The room is gigantic. The table must be twenty feet long and mostly empty. Ocher, Senor Gomez, Senora Rosita Gomez, and Manny are gathered at one end of the massive table.

"The vaqueros are out at the surrounding ranches and hills gathering horses for a drive after the first of the year," Tyler Gomez explains as he assumes his position at the head of the table. "It is only Manny, my oldest and dearest friend, and my wife Rosita. You are privileged," Tyler says smiling toward Rosita. "Rosita sent the kitchen people to visit their family in Mexico City since there are only the three of us. As you will see, she does not need any help."

Sometimes a person doesn't know if he's more tired or hungry. In this case, hunger wins out. Ocher's taste in cooking is simple. Growing up in the Philippines, it was rice with something, or beans with bacon when he cooks. Corina's foods are too hot for his tastes. Rosita Gomez introduces him to food that he could never have imaged - spicy, sweet, sour and mighty good. Rosita smiles her approval as Ocher takes a second helping.

The mood is relaxed and Ocher feels at ease. He'll sleep well, knowing that he's well protected and among friends.

He sleeps the sleep of the dead, awakes rested. The air is filled with the grays of false dawn when he awakes. Coffee and fried bread filled with honey start the day. Thinking to himself, Ocher muses, *If I die today, my last two meals are the ones I would want in Heaven.*

Ocher is standing by a holding corral looking over some mighty good ponies when Tyler walks up next to him. "Good morning Senor Ocher, I trust you slept well and are enjoying the hospitality of our humble hacienda."

"I couldn't feel more at home and I've never enjoyed better food."

"We are enjoying your company. You are welcome to stay. But, why are you here?"

"It's said among many that if I want to learn about horses there's only one place to go. So I have come to learn from the best."

"You are too kind, senor. I know some small things about horses and will gladly share that with you. The vaqueros, they know the horses. The rest of my men are not here. We have only Manny. You are welcome to stay but my men will be bringing in new horses in the fall. That is the time to learn, my friend. Come back in late summer. We will cull the herd, trail break the remainder and then drive them to the west to sell."

Ocher ponders the news, "Patron, I will be back in late summer when the horses arrive. I would beg to take advantage of your hospitality for one more day to let my horse rest and then I will go."

"You are welcome here anytime, senor." Tyler says, shaking Ocher's hand.

Ocher spends the day just loafing and talking with Manny. The two men discuss horses and food but mainly horses. Manny is a Yaqui Indian and speaks about the desert as if it were full of food, medicine and much wonder. Ocher cherishes the thought of learning from Manny about the desert.

Manny suggests a trail that heads northeast from the hacienda through the hills, ending in Laredo, Texas. A ride with plenty of water holes and scenery. Ocher decides to take Manny's advice and ride through and enjoy the country.

The next morning after breakfast and thanking Tyler and Rosita for their hospitality, Ocher walks to the barn. Manny has saddled the Pinto. Ocher says his goodbye to Manny and steps into the saddle.

Rosita, standing next to Tyler, stops him as he passes the kitchen door. She hands Ocher a parcel that truly is big enough to need a pack horse and says, "Just in case you get hungry."

She smiles and goes inside before he can say anything more.

Chapter Twenty-Four

The ride to Laredo is pleasant and very tasty. He still has food when he arrives in Laredo, around midnight of the fourth day. The Pinto is done in and so is Ocher.

Ocher finds a place to bunk. The small but clean room is all the exhausted man needs. Too tired to sleep, he rests until the town begins to make morning noises. There's still a little food left from Rosita. He'll save that for the trail. So Ocher goes to look for someplace to have breakfast. Adjacent to the rooming house, there's a small cantina that looks favorable and busy. He's in no hurry for breakfast, but he really wants some coffee.

It's the same everywhere, Taiwan, Hong Kong, Tokyo and Laredo, Texas. Young men feel the need to prove themselves. There are three of them, one on the porch and two standing in the street with their backs against the porch supports. Three is not a good number. With three, there's always the need of two to meet the approval of one. Also it's odd that three, fairly well-dressed able men are loafing around this time of the morning. It isn't Sunday and cowhands usually don't get into town 'til Saturday night. It would appear this trio is working on a reputation. They think that this is going to be easy, especially since Ocher isn't wearing a gun. The two youngest are going to instigate the fun while the older one will remain back to judge the intensity of the intimidation. The two instigators have practiced the attack. They've done this before.

When Ocher moves toward the porch, the two leaners stand and position themselves about two feet apart, not allowing space to pass between them. One is left-handed and one is right-handed, their positioning leaves their gun hands free and on the outside of the trap. Not wanting to disappoint the effort, Ocher approaches the well-rehearsed scenario.

Ocher is half a pace from the two men when the left-handed one raises his right arm in an effort to place his hand on Ocher's chest, so Ocher can't walk through the trap and spoil the planned activity. As the would-be ruffian's arm comes up, Ocher strikes the forearm with the edge of his hand. The strike shift's the momentum slightly away and exposes the young man's throat. Ocher folds his thumb into his hand and strikes him in the Adam's apple, not too hard, no need to crush his throat, just trouble him some.

The hand strike carries Ocher slightly past the men. The other cowboy's left side is completely exposed, allowing Ocher to strike the cowhand in the left kidney. The young man reacts by reaching back with his left hand to assess the damage. Ocher takes the offered arm and, with one motion, pins the arm between the shoulder blades, spins the cowboy around and walks him headlong into the support beam of the cantina's porch.

Out of the corner of his eye, Ocher notes that a horse and rider have stopped to watch the scuffle. He senses no threat from the man on horseback. Now to the man on the porch.

The older cowboy, the one on the porch, isn't looking at Ocher, but seems to be looking past him. He shows his open hands.

Ocher, picking up his sweat-stained cowboy hat speaks to the man on the porch. "Get 'em out of here."

Conceding the victory, the man lowers his hands, "Yes, sir."

Ocher turns to face a tall, leathery looking man on a gray spackled roan aiming a Navy Colt in the general direction of the cantina's front porch. The man's tanned vest is open just enough to see a Texas Ranger Badge.

"Thanks for watching my back, Ranger."

"Looks to me as if you didn't need much help."

"Thanks anyway. Least I can do is buy you breakfast."

"On a Ranger's salary, can't afford to turn down a free meal."

The cantina's crowded with working people, and ranchers but not any hung-over cowhands.

The two sit in the corner away from the windows and order.

Coffee comes before they even speak. "I'm Holt Sturdevant." He holds out a weathered hand and they shake.

"Ocher Jones."

"Glad to meet you, Ocher Jones. Do you happen to know those three young guns you braced this morning?"

As Ocher lathers butter on a hand-size biscuit, he replies, "Never saw them before. Just some young boys trying to earn a reputation."

Holt considers his words very carefully, "Wouldn't call them boys, but you're right about trying to earn a reputation. Those three came out of an orphanage back east right after the war. The older one is Billy Hawes. The one you walked into the post is Ford Carnes. The youngest of the bunch is Theo Jenks. We've been watching them pretty close for 'bout a year, don't have positive proof about anything yet. They don't ride for anybody but always seem to have money. Young, cocky, and stupid don't live long out here. You watch your back, Ocher. They won't let go of being bested, especially you without a gun."

Ocher nods, "Thanks. What brings you to these parts, if you don't mind me asking?"

"Headed out to west Texas. Heard there's some trouble brewing. Might also be some boys I'm hunting."

"Wouldn't happen to be the Double LL, would it?"

"Now how would you know that?"

"Just left there a while back. I brought their foreman to the ranch after he got shot in the back. Lewis Livingston owns the spread and some fella named Boyd's trying to take the place. That about right?"

"I don't know all the details but sounds about what I heard. Jones, you got some place to be?"

"Nope. Thought I might ride along with you. I owe you one, Ranger."

The newly acquainted pair ride out an hour later both watching their back trail. Ocher recounts the details of the shooting, and both of the run-ins with the High Range hands, leaving only a little out.

"Holt, people like Boyd are like slugs. They leave a trail of slime wherever they go. I thought his trail might be pretty interesting to the law. I just didn't know who the right people were to follow that trail. Folks like the Livingston's are worth the time and effort to help. Boyd and his kind are not."

"Ocher, I have an inkling that this is the bunch, that a lot of folks are looking for. The descriptions and the way they operate sound very familiar. Don't want to jump ahead, but it could be, just could be."

Holt isn't going to say any more. And as curious as Ocher is, this is not someone to push. In due time, he'll tell the tale. The riding and conversation are easy and they probably would have continued through the night, but agree that they might need fresh horses later. The pair stop, make camp and share what's left of Rosita's food.

Holt offers, up through a mouthful, "Yep, this has to be Rosita Gomez's cooking. I'd ride across the whole Southwest to eat at her table. She must think pretty highly of you Ocher. She never fixed me a tote." Taking a sip of coffee, Holt continues, "Sounds to me like you're mixing with some mighty nice folks. I seen what you done to those cowhands, but out here there's some fighting that won't be done close in. Don't mean to give advice but you might get a long gun, just in case."

"That's good advice. What do you carry as a saddle rifle?"

"The new 50-70 Sharps. Best long range gun I know of. Takes a bit of getting used to, but a mighty fine gun. Kicks a might."

"Speaking of shooting," Ocher says, using the flow of conversation. "Any shooting goin' on at the Double LL?"

"None that I heard of. Those are tough folks in that country. They shoot back. If there's trouble it'll be of a different kind. Mostly intimidation of one sort or the other. If there's gun play I'd have heard about it pretty quick."

The conversation lags and both men move away from the small fire. After setting aside the coffee pot, they settle in. A man learns to sleep light out in the open. They rest more than sleep and are well gone from camp by sunup.

At about noon while watering the horses, Holt remarks, "If Boyd's crew is watching the ranch we may or may not be able to sneak in. I see no reason to try and sneak by anybody watching. Not worth the effort."

Ocher gives it some thought, "I agree. No need to go through Pine Creek. Let's ride in from the south, straight into the Ranch."

Chapter Twenty-Five

The two trail weary men arrive just before sunset, coming in from the west behind the barn with the sun at their backs. On the way in they see a small camp just off the trail, with two pitiful looking cowhands that Ocher doesn't recognize. The men don't attempt to stop them from riding in. The Ranger and Ocher are surprised with the lack of activity. There's always something on a ranch that needs fixing, moving or feeding. None of that activity is evident.

"Slow and easy. Something ain't right." Ocher remarks as he dismounts and cautiously moves around the shady side of the barn. Holt follows. There's no one, no hands nor the Livingstons in sight. Ocher motions the Ranger toward the back of the house just as Amanda walks out.

Ocher moves out of the shade to let her see him and she waves him toward the house. "Glad to see you, but a lot of things have happened since you left. Come on in," Amanda says, leading them into the house.

The Ranger can see that there's no apparent danger and follows Amanda and Ocher into the kitchen, where Lewis is settled at the table. Coffee is already being poured as Holt enters. Both Ocher and Holt remain standing.

Stacey nods to the Ranger. As she looks at Ocher her eyes soften and she takes a deep breath. "Hello, Ocher."

Ocher notices the look but doesn't know what to make of it. "Stacey."

"I'll be right back," Stacey says as she hurries from the room.

Amanda glances at Ocher, then smiles.

Ocher remains confused.

"Lewis, Amanda, this is Holt Sturdevant, Texas Ranger. What's happened? Where is everybody?"

Lewis sits his coffee down, "First, money was wired from San Francisco, to pay the note. Thanks. That's what started it all. I guess Boyd refused to accept the fact that he couldn't buy the ranch, so he's decided to try and take it. We got word from town, from Boyd's banker, that the note had been paid, so I thought that maybe Boyd would back off. I sent the boys out, in pairs, to check on the stock. Boyd's people roped and dragged Beaver and Dolan through the brush and almost killed them. Shredded the hide off 'em. They're over in the bunk house all salved up.

The rest of the hands were told they would get the same treatment if they stayed. Now it's just me to tend the stock. Even if I could, Boyd's got all of the trails being watched and won't let me get out. He won't even let the women go get Doc Simpson. I may own this place, but looks like Boyd's going to keep us locked in here until we give up. Stacey, Amanda and me have been tending to the stock the best we can."

Holt, not being shy by nature, steps right into the conversation, "Glad to meet you folks, sorry it's under these circumstances. I can order those boys off of the Double LL, but that won't get you much. Sounds to me that this Boyd character will run off anybody you hire, and I can't stay forever. So, I'll try to persuade Boyd to leave you alone. Could happen, but......."

Stacey returns to the kitchen wearing a yellow ribbon in her hair, accompanied by a big smile.

The only person in the kitchen who isn't smiling is Ocher, now more confused than ever.

Ocher sips his coffee very slowly as he ponders the situation, of the ribbon and the situation around the ranch. The ribbon confusion will wait. "Holt, leave the boys out there to watch the ranch, I'm going to go talk with them after dark. Maybe some polite conversation will change some minds."

The kitchen gets very quiet. Lewis, Amanda and Stacey remain still, waiting for Holt to answer.

Holt swirls the dregs of his coffee in his cup before sitting it down. "Sometimes there's a fine line between what's right and what the law sees as right. Ocher, don't make me decide where that line is."

Stacey starts supper. Lewis, Ocher and Holt catch up on the chores. Amanda feeds and tends to Beaver and Dolan.

"What's all this smiling about over the yellow ribbon, Holt?"

"You could be in a dire situation, young man," Holt responds.

"Tread lightly, Ocher," Lewis says from one of the stalls.

Ocher can't see Lewis but Lewis's voice doesn't sound threatening.

"Will someone please explain this to me?" Ocher almost yells in exasperation.

Holt laughs, "Well, Ocher, it's an old cavalry custom. An eligible young lady gives her scarf or bandana to an eligible young man to wear. If he accepts the scarf, and wears it, he's saying, 'I got a girl. I ain't available'."

Lewis, now leaning on the stall, arms folded on the top rail says. "You came into the kitchen wearing her scarf."

"I didn't know the custom," Ocher says.

"Ignorance is no excuse," Lewis says, smiling.

"I continue." Holt says. "If the young man wears the scarf signifying his status as unavailable, well, the young lady reciprocates by wearing a yellow ribbon in her hair signifying that she is unavailable."

"Sounds to me like you're courting my daughter," Lewis says, the smile gone from his face.

Ocher doesn't know what to say. The dinner bell sounds, allowing Ocher to escape for the moment from the two men in the barn. Ocher's normally organized world is suddenly in a state of bewilderment. He heads to the house, but does not remove the bandana from his neck.

Lewis and Holt follow Ocher toward the aroma of supper.

Holt obviously enjoying the home cooked meal, chimes up, "Mrs. Livingston, this is some of the finest grub, I mean food, I've ever had. Now I have two places to look forward to visiting."

"Thank you, Holt, the other one must be Rosita Gomez. I've sat at her table and I agree. Rosita's cooking is almost as good as mine." They all laugh, some of them needing it more than others.

Just before sunset Ocher walks about half a mile from the ranch to the foothills, a burlap sack in his hands, and gathers something up that he'll need in his conversations with Boyd's men. He returns to the ranch, leaving the sack, in the shade, while he goes back into the kitchen.

Chapter Twenty-Six

It's full dark but before the moon comes up. Ocher and Holt are ready to go. "Holt, glad to have you along, I don't intend to put you in a position to uphold the law. Just stay within listening range." The two men know where the southernmost camp is, as they had passed it on the way into the ranch. After a couple of miles of easy walk, the men see the fire. Ocher stops the Ranger and whispers, "Wait here while I make some preparations. Hold this bag, but not too close to your body."

There are two of them, one asleep and one supposed to be standing guard. Ocher, like a cat, comes up behind the one on guard and applies a choke hold, just enough to render him unconscious. A rap to the temple of the other one and Ocher can take his time with the preparations. Staking both of them out, he calls for Holt. The Ranger walks into the campsite with the sack and just smiles. Ocher stands up, "You ready?" Holt nods.

Ocher cuts a small forked stick and sharpens the prongs, then heats the prongs in the fire. He then applies the heated prongs to the arm of the stacked out cowboy, the man furthest from the fire.

"Holt, douse the other one with some water. I want him to watch this."

As they both come around, Ocher dumps a rattlesnake out of the burlap bag. Both cowboys and Holt see the snake at the same instant. The variety of reactions is priceless. The cowboy who's been burned by the forked stick realizes, or so he thinks, he's been snake bit. The other cowboy can see two bleeding puncture wounds and assumes that his partner has been bitten.

Holt draws his gun.

"Don't shoot. The shot will alert the others." Ocher states as he walks over to the Ranger and whispers, "There's no fangs. I pulled them out."

"You what?" he says, holstering his Colt.

Ocher with a calm, determined, and straight face turns to the one with the supposed snake bite, "You're gonna die and your friend over there's gonna get to watch. When you're gone, and if we don't get the information we want, I'll turn the snake on him. Do you understand?"

The snake bite victim is fanatic, "Please help me. What do you want?"

Ocher remains stoic and in complete control, "Simple, just some information. Tell me about Boyd and those that came with him. Who shot Woody and who dragged my friends through the brush? You tell me that and, well, at least one of you can ride out of here. Chances are slim, the longer you hesitate, that both of you ride out."

The snake bite victim suddenly becomes eager to share.

He tries to look at his mortal wound and not cry, "Boyd, the Le Favre Brothers, Gaston and Charles, and Arnold Pennington, they all came here together. They knew each other during the war. Boyd had money, don't know how. He seems to manage the operation, but they're all part of it. Pennington's the worst of the bunch. They're all crazy and greedy but Pennington's the worst. From what I've heard the Sterling Brothers were killed after they signed the ranch over. Don't know who did the killing, could have been any of that bunch. Boyd hired on some hands, six of us. At the beginning, he bought cattle to start building up the herd. The six of us worked the ranch, but we rarely saw Boyd's people. Then cattle and horses start showing up with all kinds of brands. We didn't question anything. We rode for the brand. Mister, please help me, I'm feeling awful. Just do something about this bite."

Ocher answers with a grim look, "Soon, keep talking."

The scared cowboy continues as the sweat begins to roll down his face, "Boyd wants to own the whole valley, but hasn't got the cattle sense to run it. He ain't a cattleman. He's just crazy. As far as Woody's concerned, Pennington did the shooting. At least he bragged about it. The Le Favre's did the dragging. Please help me."

Ocher now satisfied, "You get enough Holt?"

The Ranger is just able to conceal his smile, "Yep."

Ocher walks over to the snake bite victim and cuts him loose from the stakes and does the same for the other cowhand. He does nothing about the bite but picks up the heated stick and shows it to the snake bit cowboy.

The snake bit cowboy wants to say more but, "I'll be," is all he can muster. That's his only response, but that's not what's written on his face. Even in this firelight, revenge is on his mind. Not here, not now, but sometime soon. He trembles with anger and rage.

Holt steps just far enough into the firelight for both cowboys to see the Ranger Badge. "Boys you've got just enough time to get on your horses and be out of my jurisdiction before the sun comes up. If you go back to the High Range and warn Boyd, I'll arrest you for accessory to murder and you'll be hanged. I won't use a heated stick, just a strong rope. You understand?"

The cowboy without the snake bite responds, "I reckon we just needed an excuse. Thanks, Ranger." The snake bite victim glares but says nothing.

The other two camp sites are easy to find and the same scenario plays out at both sites without the snake, just Ocher's stealth and a Texas Ranger Badge. Nothing additional is learned. By sunup Boyd is without any cowhands. Ocher and the Ranger are bone weary as they ride back to the Double LL.

Over good coffee, Holt speaks up, "Reckon I can tell you now. Right at the end of the war there was a Union Major named Thompson. He and three of his soldiers accumulated a small fortune in gold, silver and jewels stolen from anybody and everybody they could rob and kill. The whole damned army's been looking for that bunch for years. The major and his boys had their own war going on with both North and South. Some pretty evil folks. This sounds like them. I've been on and off their trail since I was mustered out. If your game, let's finish this coffee and mount up. I'd like to visit our friend Boyd over at the High Range."

The Livingston's are more than gracious and serve a quick breakfast with the coffee.
Lewis asks, "What are you going to do Holt?"
"Ocher and I are going over the High Range. By tomorrow you should be able to ride your spread without interference." Looking across the table he says, "Lewis do you have a shot gun and can we borrow it?"
"I've got a matched pair of Henrys. Will that do?" he says with obvious pride.
Holt says as he gets up from the table, "Ocher, I'd feel a bit more comfortable if you carried one of the Henrys."
Everybody in the room is caught slightly off guard when Ocher takes the Henry, checks the breech, loads the shotgun, winks and walks out the kitchen door.

Chapter Twenty-Seven

With the benefit of a full belly and some good strong coffee, the two men are prepared for the pending confrontation. Lewis insists on coming along. After all, the shotguns are his. It takes some convincing but the ranch owner finally agrees to stay home. Just in case the Boyd Gang comes to get even.

Ocher is already in the barn when Holt steps into the shade and starts to saddle up. After throwing on the saddle blanket, he pauses. "You're pretty handy, but these men are different than most. They don't abide by any rules. Their only rule is survival. Killing either one of us, or both, wouldn't inconvenience them a bit. Pennington is the worst. He has no allegiance to anybody. He just tolerates the rest of the bunch. He rides for himself."

Ocher doesn't sense any fear in the Ranger, just caution. He nods in understanding, steps into the saddle and follows Holt out of the barn.

They don't ride straight in, but stop just below the rim of a mesa to scout out the layout of High Range. Holt reaches into a saddle bag, produces a ship's spy glass and methodically studies the scene below.

"There's nothing moving around down there. Could mean that they're waitin' for us to come in. Not likely though. Don't think anybody's to home. Look east just below horizon. Riders kicking up a dust cloud, headed toward town. Need to check the ranch just to be sure."

The two men approach the High Range main house with great caution. The Pinto remains calm and shows no signs that there's anybody in hiding. There's no smoke coming from the kitchen chimney. The horse corrals are empty and there's no activity that would be normal for a ranch. The place has been abandoned.

The front porch of the frame house has collapsed at one end. The roof of the barn is showing the sky through the holes. Several of the corral posts are broken and the poles are lying in the dirt. A quick look into the bunk house reveals that the hands have been sleeping outside because one of the back walls has collapsed. The ranch shows the same level of disregard as the range does.

Holt brushes away the flies with his hat. "This place's worse than Andersonville. No wonder the hands were looking for an excuse to leave."

Ocher doesn't understand the 'Andersonville' comment and doesn't ask.

The look on the Ranger's face is one of disgust and disbelief as he looks around the place. "The only fresh tracks are headed in the same direction as that dust cloud, toward town." He starts his horse in that direction.

Holt and Ocher ride parallel to the dust cloud toward town. Holt moves across the trail several times studying the sign. "Something odd here. There are four riders. Three are leading a spare horse. The fourth rider isn't. My guess is the fourth rider has an outfit hidden behind us somewhere. If history repeats itself, they'll divide up what's at the bank and ride out in separate directions."

They follow the sign straight to Pine Springs, stopping at the edge of town. "Ocher, I'll head straight in. You go around and we'll meet at the bank. I'd like to take 'em alive, but that's up to them. Be careful of Pennington."

"How will I know Pennington?" Ocher says.

"You'll know," is Holt's response.

Holt goes straight down the main street to the bank, while Ocher cuts around the back of town through the outhouses, garbage dumps and clothes lines heavy with wash, to come up on the opposite side. In theory, this should cut off any means of escape, if in fact the men are in the bank. Ocher and Holt rein in at the front of the bank at almost the same instant. Four men step out. A man of over three hundred pounds, dressed in a suit showing sweat rings, tobacco juice, food stains and holding two carpet bags is first. Slightly behind the big man are two men that appear to be mirror images of one another. The fourth is the one to fear, a tall lanky man, lurking just behind the others, using them as a shield, his eyes searching the scene for advantage, not for the group but for himself. His stone cold look is the look of an animal laying in ambush waiting for the right instant to strike out.

Holt draws his Navy Colt, taking control of the situation, "Drop those satchels and put your hands in the air."

The fat man tosses his bags at Holt's horse while the twin brothers draw down on the Ranger. The two born together die together. Hard to say if it's the Rangers Colt or the Henry, but the result is death. In that instant, the tall lanky man sees his opportunity, fires one quick shot, turns and runs down the alley opposite of where Ocher sits the Pinto. The big man has no pistol so he puts his hands in the air. Ocher starts to wheel the Pinto around to follow the tall man when he notes that Holt's bleeding from his upper right arm and his hand gun is lying in the street. The man with his hands in the air notes the same thing and starts toward the Colt. Ocher is off his horse in an instant and steps in front of the slovenly man.

The two men are now facing each other. The man, assumed to be Boyd, is half a head taller than Ocher's five foot ten, and outweighs him by at least a hundred pounds. His size and swagger reflect the confidence of someone who's bullied his way through life. Boyd expects to deliver a quick and painful beating to the younger man, grab the Colt and kill the Ranger. He swings an anvil sized hand at Ocher's head, but to his surprise, the punch misses. Too late he realizes that he's made an error in judging his opponent.

That error's apparent when he feels his ribs break as a result of a single punch. The sound causes even Holt to wince.

Holt, holding his bleeding arm, says, "Don't kill him. The Union Army wants him alive."

The big man is game. Even with broken ribs, he tries to grab the younger man. Ocher calmly moves aside, delivering a punch to the belly. The bigger man reacts and bends over. Up to this point, Ocher's remained calm and detached about the fight, now he takes a bit of revenge. With a knife hand strike to the collar bone, the confrontation ends. With a broken right collar bone and broken left ribs there's no fight left in Boyd. He collapses on his butt in the street.

Ocher approaches the man sitting in the street. "Boyd, if that Ranger wasn't here I'd break every bone in your body and then drag you out into the desert and leave you. If you ever get out of prison and cross my path, I'll kill you for what you did to my friends out at the Double LL." Boyd sees the resolve of his attacker. With his good arm and using his boot heels, he tries to push himself backwards away from Ocher.

Holt steps over, "Damned bullet just grazed me but my whole arm went numb." Grabbing Boyd by the scruff of his sweat soiled shirt, Holt howls, "Get up."

While Doc Simpson patches up Holt, Ocher sends telegrams to the Army at Fort Stockton and the Texas Rangers in Austin. When he returns to the jail, Doc is working on Boyd. "What did you hit him with, a fence post? I didn't think a man could break bones like this with his bare hands." He looks at Ocher for an answer, but none is offered.

"Ocher, as soon as the Doc gets through fussing with my arm, I'm going after Pennington. I suspect you'll want to finish what you started? I'd rather have you with me. I can only imagine what you'll do if you catch him without me being there."

Ocher steps toward Boyd. "Where is he headed and where did he hide his outfit?"

Boyd has gotten some of his confidence back and just laughs.

"Doc, why don't you and Holt go out to the office for a minute and let me ask Mr. Boyd that question again. Doc, don't go too far. You'll be needed again."

The blood drains from Boyd's face before the Doc and Holt clear their seats. He whimpers, "Arizona Territory." Almost in tears, he stammers. "He's headed into the Territory. He hid a pack horse just above that old wind mill. Now get away from me."

"Ocher, we'll need extra horses and grub. I'm sure Livingston will provide you the horses and I'll get our supplies here in town. Meet me at the wind mill. We'll pick up his trail from there."

Ocher rides to the Livingstons where Lewis picks out a couple of excellent range horses. The stop at the Double LL is quick. Even so, Amanda manages to cook up a batch of corn fritters. "They'll keep. They're real good dipped in this honey." Ocher doesn't see Stacey standing on the porch looking after him as he rides off.

Chapter Twenty-Eight

Water is the key, you have to go where it is and avoid where it isn't.

At the wind mill, Holt is onto Pennington's trail without difficulty. "He's headed to Turkey Well. From there he can follow several known trails. It'll be after dark when we get there and cutting sign with no moon, we'll be guessing. Might as well save the horses."

Every couple of hours and when there's a bit of shade the men change mounts. They take the time to wipe out the horse's mouth with a wet handkerchief and get a sip of water for themselves.

During one of the breaks Ocher asks. "What are his choices?"

Holt takes a sip from his canteen, places the cord back over the pommel. "North toward Colorado, not much water that a way, South toward Mexico even less water or West into Apache Territory, more water and a lot more risk, especially a man alone. We'll know come first light."

Everything and everybody heads to water in this desert. A body has to be very cautious when riding up to a water hole. The reception may be hostile. Holt and Ocher stop and dismount about a half a mile out from Turkey Well. After scouting the well, a water seep that's been dug out, they approach on foot. There's a fresh fire pit and enough sign to indicate a recent, lone visitor.

They tend to the horses first, fill the canteens, a coffee pot and drink their fill. Not wanting to discourage the wildlife in the area with a human's scent they move away from the water several hundred yards, make coffee and have some corn fritters. They agree to a routine of two-hour watches through the night. This is close enough to Apache Territory. No use getting careless.

By sunup the pursuers have had rest, watered the horses, brewed coffee and eaten cold biscuits. They're on Pennington's trail, due west into the Territory.

Holt has the advantage of local knowledge. Pennington's travel is being dictated by going from one known water hole to the next. The recent rains have created small tanks and seeps of water that Holt knows about. The extra water will spare the horses. By crisscrossing Pennington's trail, by sunset the Ranger and Ocher have been able to reduce the fleeing man's lead by half.

Riding slowly so no dust is kicked up by the horses, they arrive at a small seep of water collecting at the base of a rock formation. The formation sits overlooking a wide desolate valley. Pennington's trail reveals he's on the other side of this same valley, about 10 miles ahead. Both parties are facing a formidable crossing the next day. The next water for Pennington will be up and over the barren mountains in his path. The passage will be difficult. Holt and Ocher will take an easier route by cutting through the foothills. With luck, by late afternoon the next day they'll catch the outlaw.

At the nooning they decide against coffee, just water. Then they continue in the unrelenting sun, heat and dust, ending the day in a small arroyo after filling the canteens and moving away from the well.

"Still can't get used to this," Ocher says taking a sip of the last of his coffee.

Holt has been around Ocher long enough to know he's not much on talking. So he waits, giving Ocher a chance to continue.

"Water. Where I was raised, water was a different problem. It rained most of the time. The humidity you could bathe in and mud....lots of it," Ocher says looking up at the stars.

Holt taking a chance. "Where would that be?"

"The Philippines. I was raised in the jungle. A lot different than here."

"Do you want to go back?"

"No. Never!"

Holt senses that Ocher may end the conversation. He stops questioning Ocher.

Tough to do when you're a law man and you ask questions for a living.

"In the jungle most of the predators are jungle animals, from ants to cats. And ambush animals are always close by and hidden. Not so much here." As a coyote sings his song in the distance, Ocher stops talking.

"That's a coyote, not an Indian," Holt offers.

"How can you tell?"

"No echo. A man's call will echo. A coyote's won't. If it had an echo, the coyotes couldn't communicate. They'd be confused by the echoes," Holt responds, hoping Ocher will continue to talk.

Ocher remains quiet. Holt bides his time.

"I like the openness of the desert. I mean the mountains with their trees, are not bad. But I like the wide open desert. In the jungle you can't see ten feet. And the stars, you can't really take it all in." Ocher points to the heavens with his chin. "I traveled some with a Crow Warrior, Ojos. He told me about the Indians. What warriors they are. They understand tactics, camouflage, pursuit and retreat. Better to have them as friends than enemies," Ocher says quickly realizing he may have offended Holt.

"You're right about not wanting the Indians as enemies. We've already burned that bridge. They've withdrawn to their own nations because they trust their own. It's too bad too," Holt says sensing that the conversation has ended.

The coyote sings for a couple minutes more. Ocher stands, takes a canteen and walks to the edge of the arroyo to stand the first watch.

The next day everything changes. Buzzards are circling something lying on the desert floor. Holt uses his spyglass. "Looks like a horse."

They ride toward the vultures. "It's a horse, one of Pennington's, with a broke leg." Holt scatters the birds. "That tears it, now every Apache within one hundred square miles will know that he's out here. They'll find our sign too. He's headed to the Mouse Tank, same as us. Can't leave him out there alone."

Ocher points to a dust trail running parallel to Pennington's trail. "Do you think we can catch him before they do?"

Holt looks at Ocher, for the first time with fear in his eyes. "Let's hope so."

They check the horse for anything useful, find an extra canteen and leave for the Mouse Tank.

Chapter Twenty-Nine

All trails, at least in this part of the desert, lead to the Mouse Tank. The tank is a natural collection reservoir that retains water year round. Control the approaches to the tank and every living thing comes to you. The Apaches know where the lone rider is headed and are waiting for his arrival.

The two trailing men are approaching from a different direction, but the destination for all of the parties is the same. Holt points out the faint dust trail of the Indians and the very distinctive cloud of the fleeing man. The sign's obvious. The outlaw's in deep trouble.

By walking the horses, Holt and Ocher manage to sneak up to a jumble of rocks and weeds, well short of the water tank. Stepping down, both men take the time to hobble the horses, give them a drink and ready them for a quick get a way. Just in case. Until they scout the situation they can't decide whether to attack or retreat. Holt takes his spyglass and very slowly takes to the high ground afforded by the pile of rocks. Ocher follows.

There are seven Apache braves and Pennington. They've stripped him bare, tied him to a cactus, staked open his legs and have started a fire between his thighs. Even at this distance Ocher and Holt still can hear his piercing screams. They melt back down below the ridge.

For the first time since their meeting, Holt seems a bit unnerved as he speaks, "He probably deserves what he's getting and I'm not sure how to stop it. We can probably get a couple of them but not all. That won't help Pennington. Let me think on it a minute."

Ocher removes his bandana and wipes his weary face, "Give me that Sharpes and three shells will ya? Then get ready to ride. I'm about to spoil their fun and I don't think those Apaches will be none too happy about it. Pennington's already a dead man, I'm just gonna try and end the torture and that screaming."

Holt hands over the Sharpes. He's not completely surprised as he remembers the ease in which Ocher handled the shotgun. "That's over twelve hundred yards. You sure?"

Remembering all the lessons from Able Jones. Ocher says, "I make it about twelve hundred and ten yards, no wind, just the heat waves coming off the desert. Pennington's about six foot two. That makes the target area about twenty six inches by eighteen inches, a tough shot but not impossible."

They snake back to the crest of the ridge. Ocher lays down the Sharpes and covers the exposed metal with his bandana. It's hot to the touch and he doesn't want any reflections. It's dead still. The smoke from the fire rises straight up, and the elevation is about eighty feet above the festivities. Calculating all the data that's available, setting the elevation gauge, taking a deep breath, letting it half out, Ocher squeezes the trigger.

These are seasoned warriors. They recognize the hiss of the approaching high caliber slug and vanish into the surrounding desert before the .50 caliber slug hits Pennington square in the chest.

Ocher reloads than sites in on the horses. The ponies have been loosely picketed between two Joshua Trees. The first shot explodes the small desert tree and the second scatters the ponies. Ocher hands the rifle back to the ranger. "That should buy us a little time."

Holt looks at the young man with curiosity, but says nothing. They're on the only high spot for miles. The small band of Indians will know exactly where the shot came from. The braves will also know the only escape route. Not wanting to stand on ceremony, Ocher and Holt mount up quickly and leave.

With a few minutes head start, maybe, and with no choice of direction, they head toward water. The only way out is the way they came in. The mouse tank isn't available and it's too far to water any other way.

The small scouting party read the sign left by Ocher and Holt and move to cut off any chance of escape. The Indians make no effort to reduce the dust trails. They've broken into three obvious groups. There's dust to the north and to the south, keeping the pair contained. There's also a sign of someone behind, eliminating retreat. The only unanswered question is how many are moving ahead to cut off the approach to the next water?

Holt appears calm about the situation. At the first available shelter, he stops. Holt steps down and pulls the Sharpes from the saddle scabbard. "Ocher, discourage our friends back there. That should get us a little more time to think our way out of this. I'll tend to the horses."

Ocher can see two riders. He fires two rounds in the general direction. The result is they duck for cover. He waits until the dust settles then fires two more shots. The Indians will now have to be a bit more cautious about coming too close. As Ocher steps off the boulder he's using for cover, he says, "Holt I have an idea."

Chapter Thirty

"They've given up their advantage," Ocher says with more calm than he feels. "By trying to herd us, they've split up and given us an opportunity. The question is what do we do?"

Holt doesn't understand, "Opportunity? All right go on."

"Two questions: How did they split up? What's the shortest way out of the territory?"

The Ranger thinks over the questions. "If it was me, I'd have sent one man ahead to control the water hole. Using Pennington's horse and his own pony he could ride hard and cut off access to the water. One man could hold us off until the rest arrive. I'd put two men driving us toward the water. You'd only need one man south of us. Only a fool would consider riding deeper into Apache Territory. That leaves three men up north, the shortest way out."

"I'd say you got it figured right. There are two back there." Ocher points with his chin. "We have to do something unexpected."

"I'm listening."

"Let's keep moving. Somewhere up ahead I'll drop off and set up an ambush. You keep going with the horses leaving a trail."

Holt hesitates only for a second. "Could work, except I'll drop off and you keep going. We're out here doing my job."

Ocher picks his words very carefully. "No disrespect. You'll just kill those two. I won't unless I have to."

Holt looks over at Ocher as he mounts up. "You're right about the killing part. In the end that might be the only way. Grab the ponies. We can use them to try a bluff."

The men ride out into the sun, heat, sand and cactus. Ocher pulls up alongside Holt and points off in the distance. "See that clump of creosote trees and brush just there? Head for that. I'll be along directly."

Ocher slides from the saddle and moves just slightly off the trail, leaving little or no sign. He locates a slight depression in the shade of a Yucca bush. He scoops out more sand making the depression just deep enough to lie in. Getting into the scooped out hole he covers most of his body with sand, leaving just enough uncovered to see the trail. In his right hand he holds a rock sling and in his left three small stones.

He can feel the riders through the ground before he sees them. Their attention's focused on the fleeing riders and they miss the small telltale sign of the ambush. The two Indians are riding about twenty feet apart, one on each side of the trail. Ocher waits for them to pass, very slowly stands, places a stone in the sling and hurls the rock at the closest brave. The second stone is in the air before the first one connects.

The first stone strikes the Apache just at the back of the head. The sound makes the other man turn his head toward the noise. As he turns the second stone hits him right between the eyes. Both of the pursuers are down. Ocher checks both of the braves. They're alive. He drags them into the depression. Leaving only the water bags and one knife, he retrieves their ponies and rides out.

Holt's sitting in what little shade the clump of bushes provides with his rifle across the lap when Ocher rides in with the two ponies. "That should give us some choices."

"What about those two?" Holt asks.

"They'll be out for a while, then it's a long walk."

"Ocher, what say we try and confuse that bunch up north? We'll use an old Indian trick, by tying some scrub brush behind those ponies. Setting 'em loose will create a couple false dust trails. We can do the same with our packhorses. If we're right that has three scouts on six different trails. Might split them apart, enough for us to sneak through."

Ocher considers the notion. "Good, don't want to have to fight our way out if we don't have to. Where we gonna meet up?"

"Due north, there's a place called Fools Canyon. From the top it looks mighty inviting, but it ain't. Once you ride in, you're trapped.

You can ride in but the only way out is to climb. Most folks don't know about the old foot trail, but I do. On the Northeast rim is a stand of Pinions. Right after it rains, water runs through there and into the valley. Come in from the east. I'll be along."

The two men start tying brush together with strips of cord made from a nearby Yucca. Working slow and steady within the hour they have four brush bundles ready to go. Holt saddles up and grabs the lead from one of the Indian ponies. "I'll head west and let him go in a mile or so. Right after dark I'll turn east. Should be there about the time the moon comes up. If we're not together by sunrise, well whoever's there, ride north."

Before Ocher can object, Holt rides off to the west, deeper into the Apache Territory. Ocher takes the lead of the remaining pony and heads northeast. Off to his left he can see the dust trails being made by the Ranger and the pony. About a mile out, Ocher releases the other Indian's pony. Within minutes there will be six dust plumes.

Not a breath of a breeze moves as the day progresses. Ocher keeps a close vigil on the other 'riders'. The other horses are not moving in a direct line. The trails meander, cutting back on themselves and stopping from time to time. If Ocher and the Pinto ride in a straight line it won't match the trails of the decoy trails. Ocher and the Pinto match the movements. No use giving away any advantage.

As the sun begins to set, Ocher can see large clouds building over the San Francisco Mountains. He thinks, *Hope that turns to rain. Tracking us will become almost impossible.*

As the light begins to fade, the slope of the terrain begins to increase. He picks a trail that will lead him east of the Pinions. At full dark he stops the Pinto, for a well-deserved rest and a drink. The lightning provides quick glimpses of the trail as they continue the climb. The air is charged with the lightning but no smell of rain.

The ground levels off, and, during a brief lightning burst, Ocher can see the stand of Pinions. He moves the Pinto to a pile of brush caught up in a Saguaro and stops. Using the lightning's illumination, he studies the rendezvous for over an hour then moves just into the trees. From his vantage point he can see the trails that'll be used to approach his position. He doesn't dismount, but sits patiently, watching. The Pinto seems to understand and doesn't move or get restless.

Chapter Thirty-One

When plans work, you feel lucky. When they go bad, they do so quickly. Ocher's sitting just inside the tree line and thinking, *Holt's plan is about to go very bad.*

The moon's just rising in the east, providing a soft background glow. The lightning in the west offers up quick bursts of intense light. If a rider's out in the open, one source of light or the other will reveal his position. No place to hide.

The moon's at Holt's face. He's moving from one hiding place to another. The fact that Ocher can see him isn't unsettling. It's the Apache warrior who's trailing the Ranger that's disturbing Ocher. Holt's checking his back trail but, from his movements, he's not making any changes to avoid detection.

A lightning flash reveals two more braves approaching on ponies from the opposite direction. This stand of pinion's going to get crowded, very soon. The Pinto's beginning to lose patience and starts to fidget. "I see them." Ocher reassures the horse.

Years of training have taught Ocher to be patient, but this whole situation's testing his patience. Ocher smiles, as he finally realizes that Holt's deliberately leading the warriors toward the hidden trail. *You old fox. Hope it works.*

And things just got more crowded. A fourth Apache just came out of the desert. He's walking, leading his pony, studying the ground in the moonlight. He hasn't seen Holt, not yet.

The lightning's right on top of the mesa now. The scene's as bright as day. Lightning strikes are hitting the rocks, trees and anything head high. Holt's heading down into Fools Canyon. The Apaches are trying to follow him and take cover. The Pinto finally has had enough and moves out from the Pinions. The Pinto's decision saves Ocher's life. Just as they move out of the trees, a lightning bolt strikes the tree where they just left. The lightning strike explodes the Pinion, filing the air with wood slivers. Ocher feels the pressure like someone pushing his shoulder. He looks down and sees a piece of the tree protruding from his chest, just under the left collar bone.

He thinks, *How odd, there's no pain.* He reaches up to remove the sliver of wood and, as soon as he touches it, the pain begins. The last thing Ocher remembers – rain has started to pour down.

Chapter Thirty-Two

Ocher's always trusted and relied on his senses. He's never questioned them, until now. He knows he's been injured. The smells, the sounds and the world around him are not making sense. The few times he escapes from sleep confuse him before he lapses back into black.

He smells coffee, but no wood fire. The ground he's sleeping on should be hard but is soft. The voices should be that of Apache braves, but he can understand the talk, or parts of it. The most confusing part is the sweet smell of lavender. No Indian or Holt has that scent. The horses certainly don't smell that good. He can't stay conscious long enough to figure all of it out.

Lavender is the key. Stacy Livingston smells of lavender. But what's she doing out here in the Territory. Ocher fights his way out of his sleep. *Have to save Stacey, she shouldn't be out here.*

Opening his eyes he looks around a room that he has seen before, but where? Not long ago he helped place Woody in this same room. Not a memory to wake up to. There's someone hovering next to his left shoulder. He turns to see the smiling face of Doc Simpson.

"Howdy, son. You're safe." The Doc gets right to the point. "You gave us a scare, but the worst is over. It would help if you had some broth or something."

Ocher thinks on it a bit and speaks. The voice is not one he recognizes. "Coffee?"

The Doctor shakes his head. "OK, but it'll have sugar in it. You'll need something other than coffee to help you gain some strength. The sugar ain't much, but it's a start. I'll speak to Amanda on the way out. Don't push too hard."

Ocher makes a feeble attempt to sit but abandons the effort as Amanda walks in.

"Hey, cowboy. Let's sit you up a bit and try a sip of this coffee." Amanda carefully moves Ocher forward and places several pillows at his back, fixes the quilt and finally hands the coffee mug to Ocher.

He nods in thanks. "My horse?"

Amanda smiles broadly. "Don't worry about that horse. He recovered from the ride pretty quick when we put him in with the mares."

Holding the mug is a challenge. Ocher manages a sip, spills a bit, frowns at the sweet taste and hands the mug back. "Not as thirsty as I thought. Can't remember much, how long?"

"Holt brought you in six days ago. You lost a lot of blood and infection has set in. You've been asleep for most of that time." She holds Ocher upright while removing the pillows and slowly lowers him back down. "It took Doc Simpson a while to realize that you had a tattoo on your upper chest, where the splinter went through. He thought it was a bruise or something until he got a good look at it. Now get some rest."

The next time he does better with the coffee, managing to get more in, than on. Coffee with sugar ruins the taste, but the Doctor said sugar will help the healing process, so he drinks it. He has only fleeting glances of Stacey. His only visitors have been Amanda and Lewis.

Over the next day he manages three full mugs of coffee, mostly milk and sugar with some coffee for color. Ocher decides to make the journey to the front porch rocker. A real test of his abilities, but he manages with Amanda's help. He's resting after making it to the rocker and being tucked in, when Stacey walks out of the barn leading the Pinto. As soon as the Pinto sees Ocher on the porch, the horse's ears prick up. Stacey leads the Pinto to the porch close enough for Ocher to stroke the horse on the nose. She let's go of the lead and the Pinto just becomes part of the gathering.

Ocher leans back in the rocker, "He seems to like you. He won't let most folks near him."

Stacey smiles rubbing the Pinto's nose, "I'm good with horses 'cause they seem to think. Cows, on the other hand, don't seem to think at all, just react."

Stacey starts to say more but stops when Holt rides into the yard. Instead she says. "I'll get you two, something to drink."

Holt steps down from his horse, strokes the Pinto. "Morning, I see you finally decided to try upright for a change. I wish I'd knowed that a splinter to the shoulder would've got this kind of attention."

Ocher takes the jibe with a smile. "Reckon I owe you for getting me back here."

Holt smiles and shakes his head and points at the Pinto with his chin. "Not likely. That mule headed Pinto of yours is the one to thank."

Stacey steps out to the front porch with two mugs of coffee. She hands each man a cup, says hello and steps back into the house. Ocher has always enjoyed Holt's company but wishes he hadn't been present when Stacey brought the coffee.

Holt takes a sip, coughs a bit. "This must be yours. It's got sugar in it. What next, you gonna be riding side saddle?"

Ocher just smiles, knowing Holt wouldn't be this casual if anything was seriously wrong. "The Pinto?"

"Yeah. When the lightning struck the Pinion, you got hit with that wee bit of a splinter. It knocked you off the Pinto. That was only the beginning. The lightning struck everything above head high. Those Apache's know bad medicine when they see it. They wanted off that mesa, pronto. Those indians abandoned their ponies and took off headed toward the valley and low ground. Then that Pinto of yours ran off all of the ponies in the middle of that storm. How he didn't get hit is beyond me."

Ocher knows that isn't the whole of the story. "The last thing I remember was you out in the open with a brave trailing you."

Holt pushes back his hat with the tip of his finger. "I was leading them Apaches down into the canyon. I told you that there's an old foot trail. I was just gonna stroll on out during the storm. When I saw the Pinto running off the ponies, I took the opportunity to find you. That piece of tree went almost all the way though, so I just pulled it out. By the time I made a quick patch, the Pinto was back. I loaded you up and off he took. That fool horse took a trail I'd never seen before. He only stopped long enough for a quick drink. Damn horse almost rode me to death."

Holt notes that Ocher's color has faded and his speech is labored, so makes an excuse. "I've got work to do, can't be taking tea with you for the rest of the day. I'll be by tomorrow before I head back to Austin."

Ocher knows there's a lot more to the story, but also knows the Ranger won't say much more.

Holt steps into the saddle. "Good thing for both of us that Pinto let us tag along with him." He turns his horse and rides back toward Pine Springs.

Amanda walks to the porch and, without asking, leads Ocher back to bed. His last thoughts are. *It makes a lot more sense now.*

The next morning Ocher gets a real treat: scrambled egg, biscuit and grits. Unfortunately it comes along with that sweet coffee. The thought of breakfast and the prospect of walking around the ranch to palaver with the hands, start Ocher's day off right. But halfway through the first bite, reality steps in. One bite of egg and the sweet coffee is all he can manage.

The move to the front porch improves Ocher's attitude, especially after the defeat of breakfast. The journey is made much more pleasant when both Amanda and Stacey accompany him on the trek. Ocher knows that Stacey's been close by as he catches a whiff of lavender now and then. He wishes for just a moment of her company.

The women retreat back into the house just as Holt and another man ride into the yard. Holt steps down but the other man does not. "Ocher, there's someone I want you to meet."

Ocher takes a hard look at the man, knowing who he is or was. The man sitting the horse is clean shaven, wearing new clothes and dry. "Step down."

The man steps down, removes his cowboy hat and steps to the edge of the porch.

"Mr. Jones, I ain't much for talking but I'll give it a go. My name is Bogart Dunsten. We've met a time or two. You showed me a kindness by not killing me when you had the chance. Things were tough after the war and I fell in with some bad company. I'd like the chance to get back my reputation. You'll be needin' a good hand."

Holt stops the man. "You don't know this part, Ocher. The Governor, for whatever reason, has granted you an unencumbered deed to the

High Range. The Army's also given you a $20,000 reward for capturing Major Thompson."

Ocher's taken aback by all of this. He hesitates while considering what to speak to first. "Please call me Ocher." He offers his hand to the cowboy.

The man takes off his roping glove and takes Ocher's hand. "My friends call me 'Bug'. I'd take it kindly if you would."

"Bug, you've seen the shape of the High Range. You get started on the place and I'll be along as soon as I'm able. Starting now, you're the foreman."

"You won't regret it, Ocher." Bug mounts up and heads for the High Range.

"Holt, I just helped you with the Thompson bunch. That should be your reward."

"I'm a Texas Ranger and that's my job. I can't take reward money. I'll be coming through here from time to time. I'll need a place to set a bit. Best get yourself a good cook, 'cause I'll take be taking my cut out in chow."

"You got a deal. I got my eye out on a good cook," Ocher smiles broadly.

"One more thing." Holt walks over to his saddle, removes a hand tooled rifle scabbard and hands it to Ocher. "Some of the Ranger's heard about that lucky shot you made on Pennington. They thought this 50-70 Sharpes might improve your shooting."

Ocher removes the buffalo gun from the buckskin scabbard and places the rifle on his lap. He turns the rifle over and looks at the hand-engraved Texas Ranger Badge inlaid with silver and gold. The barrel's a black blue color and is also engraved with a scroll pattern. He's overwhelmed and his breath catches. "Tell 'em thanks."

Holt tilts his hat to Stacey as she walks to the porch. "Hear you're a mighty good cook, young lady." He turns his horse before she can reply and rides out.

Stacy turns to Ocher. "What did he mean by that?"

Before Ocher can respond or enjoy the moment with Stacy, Beaver limps around the corner of the house. "Grubs up, the boss sent me around to help, if you need it."

Stacey gives Beaver a fleeting glare before she recovers her smile. "I'll go help mother."

Beaver watches Stacey retreat into the house, turns to Ocher. "Take it slow and easy. I'll be right here if you need to lean. Funny, I knowed that girl her whole life. Never seen her this skittish. Don't rightly know if it's you or her going away that's got her head up."

Ocher almost stumbles. "Going away?"

"Yep, in all this trouble we all forgot about it. Right after the New Year she's headed for New York City to finishing school. Finishing what I don't know, but she'll be gone for almost a year."

The walk around the house to the summer kitchen takes a little longer than usual as Ocher has to stop once to catch his breath. Everybody's at the table when they finally arrive and the two men are greeted with smiles and hellos. Ocher's place is next to Stacey. The meal's simple and he eats more than he thinks he can. He even gets the chance to have casual conversation with her. The meal and conversation end when Lewis stands. "I believe we have a ranch to run. Best get at it."

Ocher wants to help with the work, but isn't quite ready. He decides to sit out on the porch and work up the strength to walk to the corral to see the Pinto. The trip through the ranch house doesn't completely exhaust him. Feeling adventurous he doesn't stop and rest in the rocker. Forging ahead, he steps off the porch and sets a course toward the corral. In his mind it's a straight course but it's far from straight. The Pinto sees him coming and stands at the rail.

"Howdy," gasp, "partner." Ocher manages to say holding the rail with both hands.

The Pinto nudges Ocher's arm.

Ocher in a bold move lets one hand go and scratches the Pinto's nose. "Looks like it's me and you. Stacey's heading off to something called finishing school in New York."

The Pinto moves his head to redirect the scratching.

"It kinda makes me feel a bit empty. Never felt like that. What do you think I should do?" Ocher asks the Pinto.

"Makes me feel kind of empty too, Ocher," Lewis says walking out of the barn. Lewis walks over next to Ocher and places his arms on the rail. The Pinto stays in place enjoying the scratching.

"There's an old custom or maybe wives' tale out here. If you bury your baby's afterbirth under a tree on your ranch, the baby will always come back home. Don't know the truth of that but we done it. I guess it means, you have to have faith that you done enough good that your children want to be near you," Lewis says as he turns and leans against the corral.

"You aren't afraid that Stacey won't want to come back to this?" Ocher points out to the open range with his scratching hand.

"Can't say for sure. Hope she does. Got to let her have a taste for the city though. If I don't, she'll always wonder about it," Lewis says turning back around.

"Still makes me feel empty," Ocher says returning his hand to scratching.

"Ocher, we all see the way you two cow eye each other. And believe me she's tried to dig in her heels over the whole thing. Have faith, my boy. I have to. You'll have to do the same. You both need a little maturing. Tyler Gomez is a good man. It'll be your finishing school. Stacey will, hopefully, learn what's important in her life. Her mom ain't likely to let her little girl go and not come back. Patience, Ocher, patience.

"I ain't spoke that many words, well ever. I got a ranch to run. Need help getting back to the house?" Lewis finishes and looks at Ocher.

"I'll stay here a bit more then wobble back," Ocher answers.

The Pinto stands close, enjoying the attention.

"Horse, it's just you and me again. She needs to see the elephant as much as I did. Like the man said, if she don't see it... well, she'll always wonder about it. You probably know more about women than I do. There weren't any in the jungle that weren't fat and uglier than the monkeys. Stacey sure isn't either of those. Never seen her back down neither. Don't know what to do about any of this. Thanks for listening, we'll talk some more." Ocher turns and wobbles towards the house.

Chapter Thirty-Three

"Morning, Bug," Ocher says as he looks up from putting on his leather soled moccasins, making sure to put on the right one first. Bug had pointed out that a cowboy always puts on his right boot first and Ocher could see no reason that the tradition didn't apply to moccasins.

The foreman ambles out of the bunkhouse, boots in one hand and holding up his pants with the other. His cowboy hat already in place. Bug drops his boots, rubs his hands under his arm pits, warming and scratching at the same time. He takes note of the weather and the Pinto standing nearby. "Morning, Boss. Horse. I never knowed anybody who liked to run like you and that horse. You two been runnin' all over this ranch for six weeks now."

The morning ritual started the day Ocher moved to the High Range. The first week was the tough one. Ocher struggled to walk or run into the high meadows. To get back to the ranch he had to ride the Pinto bareback. Now he could run to the meadows, do his stretching, work on his hand skills and run back to the ranch with ease, the Pinto right there with him.

He loves to run, always has. Running in the jungle or on the island beaches was not too different from running in the desert. Both places have snakes, scorpions and tarantulas. In the jungle, the threat was up in the canopy. Here they're all at ground level.

His running serves two purposes. First is to rebuild his physical strength. The second gives Ocher the opportunity to learn the layout of the ranch. He now knows the patterns of the deer, rabbits, quail, and elk. He also knows the terrain, ambush points, escape routes and hide outs, if one's needed.

He's also beginning to appreciate why people come west to ranch. It sure isn't for the money. There isn't any. The beauty of the land and the satisfaction of hard work are the driving forces.

The morning run ends as the last few have, with Ocher racing the Pinto back to the corral. The Pinto pulls up just short of the gate, letting Ocher win. "You don't have to let me win every time, you know," Ocher says as he puts out some grain and hay, strokes the Pinto's nose then turns to walk toward the aroma of breakfast.

"I swear, Bug, your cooking's either getting better or I'm just getting hungrier," he says as he enters the small kitchen set up in the bunkhouse.

"It ain't my cooking that's changed, must be that running. The fact that you work hard as any two men I ever seen could mean something," Bug offers as he sets out scrambled eggs and chili with cornbread. "That should hold you for a spell."

Ocher pours coffee for them both. "We should be able to move the kitchen back into the house in a day or so. After that we can live over there."

Bug stops in mid mouthful. "You said *we* can live in the main house?"

"Yep. Is that a problem?"

"Well, Boss, I never lived in the main house afore. I'd be more to home in the bunkhouse. Besides."

Ocher starts to laugh. Bug soon follows.

"That first night," Ocher begins. "What was it you said? I ain't going in there, Ocher. Not after dark. No telling what's eating what in there."

"Yeah, I remember. I also remember you weren't too eager to go in there either."

"Glad we waited until the next morning. Building that smoke fire and smoking those critters out of there was a good idea. Can't believe the livestock that came out of that house."

"That ain't the reason for not living in there. I just never had that station in life. Living in the big house," Bug remarks as he continues eating his breakfast.

Ocher sets down his spoon. "It would be more sensible if we stayed in the same place. You gonna live in the bunkhouse when I head down to Sabinos?"

"I am. No use messing up the big house when all I need's a bunk and a stove," Bug responds.

"Ok. Let's leave the kitchen stuff here. The kitchen will need a woman's touch anyway."

"You thinkin' of a specific woman or just in general?" Bug comments, already knowing the answer.

"Mind your manners or you'll be out in the corral with that other hardheaded critter."

"That other hardheaded critter's already taken off again. He got a drink and bolted out of here," Bug notes as he points toward the empty corral.

Chapter Thirty-Four

Ocher was just reaching the top of the ladder with a bundle of split roof shingles when Bug points his hammer and mumbles though the roofing nails in his mouth. "Gonna have company." Ocher looks past Bug to see a buckboard coming up the trail from the Double LL. Bug continues, "Looks like Miss Amanda and what's that girls name again?"

"Stacey," Ocher says and starts back down the ladder, "I'm gonna wash this dust off and put on my shirt so I look presentable."

"A man's supposed to be dirty. Must be some other reason for washing," Bug says with a smile as he follows Ocher off the roof.

Amanda pulls the mule-drawn buckboard right up to the front porch of the main house, wraps the reins around the hand brake and picks up a rifle that she had leaned up against the seat. She accepts Bug's hand and starts to step down. Stacey keeps her seat until either Bug or Ocher assists her.

Ocher's across the yard at the horse trough next to the stables drying his hands on a flour sack when he notes the mules raise their heads and look up the hill behind the corral. Something's alarmed the mules. Ocher turns to look at the front porch to see Bug and Amanda looking up the hill. Stacey steps down, on her own, and is moving toward the porch. Ocher can't locate the exact spot that's alerted the mules until the covey of quail flush up. He starts to move toward the house when he hears a rifle shot and the buzzing sound of the bullet passing close by his head. His only choice is to head for the barn.

The barn affords cover from the hill side and also allows Ocher to see the sheltered side of the main house. Bug's standing in an open window and shrugs his shoulders as if to say, *"Don't know who or why."* Ocher also notes that the exposed front porch is being covered by the two women, the barrels of two rifles aimed up the hill side. The shooter on the hillside doesn't realize he's just stirred up a hornet's nest.

Ocher yells over to Bug. "Cover me, I'm going up there."

From the weeks of running, Ocher knows the terrain and every hiding place. The quail have provided an exact location. The shooter thinks he has the upper hand by having the higher ground. He does have the field of fire over the ranch yard but not on the hillside. The logical counter attack would be through the gulley and around the back of the hill. However, when the covering fire starts, Ocher is going straight up the hill. If the shooter wants to take a shot at Ocher, he'll have to stand up to get the angle. The coyote hides nailed to the barn are a testament to Bug's skill with a rifle. The shooter on the hillside doesn't realize he's lost the advantage.

Bug, Amanda and Stacey step out from the house onto the covered porch just far enough to let loose six rounds at the rock formation where the covey of quail flushed up. Before the echo of the last round dies down, Ocher's at the base of the hill. The trio's surprised by the move but sees the advantage immediately. They move out to the edge of the porch keeping the rifles aimed up the hill ready for a shot.

Ocher slowly and methodically moves from cover to cover, rock to rock, bush to bush. His shirt's still on the post next to water trough. The December sun is beginning to roast his back and neck. Six weeks ago he would've been so winded he'd had to rest by now. But with his stamina back, he's in his element, the stalk.

Ocher is high enough on the hill side to be just below and to the west of the shooter. He makes the extra effort to plan each step, the cowboy boots making progress just a bit slower. The moccasins would have been better, but, when being ambushed, preplanning is difficult. Ocher wants to get close enough to take the shooter alive. The sound of someone blowing his nose gives Ocher an estimate of distance, about twenty feet. Ten would be better. He picks up a small stone and tosses it over the shooter's head and steps out from behind the rock to make the final charge. The shooter's reaction to the sound of the stone hitting the ground is expected. He stands and wheels toward the sound.

Ocher tries to warn him not to stand but it's too late. The shots are quick but slightly off target. One bullet strikes the shooter's rifle just above the cocking lever, shattering the rifle, the butt end careening toward Ocher. Already having his fill of wood splinters, he steps back behind the boulder as the remnants of the rifle pass by. When Ocher steps out again, the shooter's fleeing up the hill. No doubt he's heading for his horse.

Just as Ocher starts up the hill after the shooter, he notes the man standing just at the top of the hill with his hands in the air. Surely Bug couldn't have gotten up the hill that quick.

Ocher walks up the hill well away from the man just in case whoever's up there starts shooting. Bug, Amanda and Stacey must see this from the porch because there haven't been any more shots.

He steps over the rise and is confronted by six Apache Warrior's on horseback, all focused on the man with his hands up. The other surprise, the Pinto standing amongst the warriors as calm as all get out.

Ocher's immediate reaction is amazement. How did he not sense or see these braves before now. The skill level to approach the ranch unseen or unheard is admirable and unsettling. He won't underestimate these men again.

The indian in the middle of the party speaks, but, even before he does, Ocher knows he's the leader. There's no eagle feathered headdress or any fancy ornamental staff. Just the carriage of the man. His air of authority and vibrancy tell the story. Ocher has no fear of the warrior or the situation. None of the men are wearing what Holt calls war paint. If these men wanted them dead, they would already be dead.

One brave slides off his pony and kicks the legs out from under the man with his hands in the air. As soon as the man's on the ground, his hands are bound behind his back with leather thongs. He immediately rolls over, but makes no attempt to sit up and has the good sense not to speak.

The leader of the party looks at Ocher and speaks. When he had spoken for a minute or so, the brave next to him speaks in English. "It has been said at the council fire that a man of much medicine will come from across the great water. This man will have the mark of the ancient warriors here." The brave places his palm on his left upper chest. Ocher's shirt is still hanging on a corral post. The men in the gathering can see the tattoo right where the man has indicated.

The leader speaks again and the brave continues to interpret the words. "The man will walk among the human beings as a friend."

Ocher can't comprehend how this warrior can know this much about him.

The talking continues. "This warrior has no clan. Let it be told at the fires that he has been chosen by the Horse Clan." The warrior, that's been speaking, slides off the bare back of his pony. He walks over to Ocher, his footsteps not making a sound. He removes a knife from a scabbard fastened around his waist by a beaded belt. Holding the knife to the sky, he speaks in English. "Let the ancient ones see this man." Exposing the palm of his right hand, he slices open the fatty part of the palm then hands the knife to Ocher.

Ocher instinctively knows what to do. How he knows is a mystery, but he knows. He makes the incision on his hand and hands back the knife. The Apache grunts his approval, grasps Ocher's hand so that the knife wounds marry. "You are now my brother. No longer will you be without a clan. Your hands will now be used for life, not death as you were trained. What name have you chosen?"

"Shiilooshe." Ocher responds.

"From our brothers the Crow Nation. Do you know the white man's word?"

"Yes. Ocher."

The Apache grunts his approval, "From mother earth. Have you another name?"

"Jones, Ocher Jones."

Ocher's new blood brother smiles, "Abel Jones?"

"Yes."

"You have chosen well. I am called by the white man 'Geronimo'."

The man on the ground sits bolt upright. His face has turned ashen and he gasps. "Dear Lord, what have I gotten myself into?"

Geronimo ignores the man on the ground as he would a tumbleweed, removes his hand from the exchange, turns and walks to the Pinto. As he rubs the muzzle of the horse, he leaves a blood stain. "You have chosen wisely, little brother." He pauses and turns to face Ocher again. "The tall buffalos are also our brothers. Do not be afraid."

Before Ocher can ask about the tall buffalos the Apaches are gone. No farewells, no fanfare, and no sound.

He turns to the man on the ground. "Where's your horse?"

The bound man looks at Ocher and points to the rim of the ridge with his chin. "My God man, that was Geronimo. I don't know of any white man that's ever been this close to Geronimo and lived to talk about it."

"Well, mister, you'll have something to talk about in prison. Now get up. Let's get going."

"To hear people talk, I would've though he was taller," the man on the ground continues.

"Mister, being tall or big doesn't make you a man. I just met a big man." Ocher leads the bound man over the rise of the hill, the Pinto trailing along. "What's your name?"

"Garrett Tubbs."

"Why did you try and ambush me?"

"You and that Texas Ranger shamed me and I don't take that from nobody, 'til now. I'll do my time and I won't come hunting you when I get out. Don't want Geronimo on my trail. Sure glad I missed."

Ocher cuts the bindings from his hands. "Saddle up, Tubbs, and remember there are still three rifles trained on you from the ranch."

"Don't worry, mister. You'll have no more trouble from me, ever."

Tubbs mounts up as Ocher walks over to the Pinto. "Well, aren't you full of surprises," he says as he strokes the muzzle of the horse, leaving an additional blood stain. "All this time I thought I had picked you."

Tubbs takes the lead as the pair ride back down the hill and into the yard of the ranch.

Chapter Thirty-Five

"Well, Garrett Tubbs, I should have guessed. You all right, boss?" Bug asks.

Before Ocher can respond, Tubbs blurts out. "Geronimo, Bug, honest to God it was Geronimo. He and your boss are blood brothers."

Ocher slides off the bareback of the Pinto and starts to speak.

But Tubbs continues. "Like magic them braves showed up. Never heard a thing. Same with him." He points at Ocher. "I never heard any of them. I've lost my edge, maybe I need some jail time. That was too close. Geronimo! Man oh man."

Bug looks toward Ocher. "So you're a blood brother of Geronimo."

Ocher still can't get a word in. Stacey sets down Ocher's rifle and steps out into the yard. "Let me see that hand. You're dripping blood all over yourself. Couldn't you just have shook hands?" She takes Ocher by the hand and walks him over to the water trough and to wash out the cut. She removes her cotton bandana from her neck, rinses it out and wraps it around Ocher's hand.

Ocher is temporarily disoriented by the fact that Stacey is holding his hand. He relishes the moment. In an effort to regain his composure, he mumbles, "We still got work that needs doing and he needs to be taken into the sheriff. Bug, you run Tubbs into town. Pick up our supplies while you're there."

Tubbs steps down from his horse and looks at Ocher. "Mister, I won't be needin' my horse for a while. You mind putting him up? I'll fetch him up in a year or two. I'll ride along with Bug into town in the wagon. I've had enough excitement for one day."

Amanda walks to the Double LL wagon, places her rifle into the scabbard. "We're headed into town. Just came by to see if you needed anything. We'll follow along with Bug just in case. That hand ok? Geronimo, don't that beat all. Lewis will want to hear all about this. We're expecting you and Bug to Christmas dinner?"

Ocher hasn't been a part of a Christmas but won't pass up any opportunity to be around Stacey before she leaves for New York. "We'll be there."

Chapter Thirty-Six

What Ocher had hoped for was a quiet day to be with Stacey and his friends. The day turned out to be the exact opposite. Garrett Tubbs has apparently spread the word about Geronimo's visit. He's now a minor attraction, but Ocher has become a celebrity. It seems like most of Pine Springs has dropped by to visit during Christmas Day. The kids wanted to see the knife cut and the men want to stand close to Ocher. Like some magic protection will wear off.

The Sheriff even shows up using the excuse to tell Ocher that Tubbs had been picked up by a U.S. Marshall and was on his way to Austin. After seeing the comings and goings at the Livingston's, he ushers everyone off the ranch so the family could at least have supper in peace.

Just before the sheriff departs, he takes Ocher aside. "It's probably a good thing that you'll be heading out of town at least for a while. Maybe by the time you get back, this will all calm down. Seeing the way you look at that gal, you'll be at the stage in the morning. See you there."

On the way through the front gate of the ranch, the Sheriff turned a wagon full of guests around before heading off toward town.

The day finally arrives. Stacey's leaving for New York City to finishing school. Ocher's headed to Sabinos, Mexico, to learn about and buy horses. The weather pretty much matches his mood, dreary and miserable.

Stacy's all dressed up in her traveling dress, yellow ribbon, parasol in hand, travel bag sitting on the porch and the derringer, that her dad had given her for Christmas, in her front pocket. She accepted the gift only after the fight.

"I don't want or need to go to finishing school," Stacey announces for the umpteenth time to her parents. "There's nothing there I want to see. It's expensive and unnecessary," she declares.

"We've already paid the money," her dad offers.

Amanda takes a deep breath, "If he's worth having he's worth waiting for. You need to see what's out there. Then you can appreciate what's here."

"But..." Stacey starts but doesn't finish. She knows her mom is right and she hasn't won this argument. No matter how hard she tries. Reaching into her pocket she feels the derringer. "The finishing school folks might frown on a sophisticated young lady toting a gun."

Her mom is ready, "Good sense, is good sense."

Ocher notes that a travel box with embossed paper and a set of pens is right at the top of the travel bag. He gave her the writing box as a Christmas present.

Ocher tries to make sense of the Christmas celebration but can't. It would have been easier to understand had it not been for all the town's folks showing up. The holiday provided him the opportunity to give Stacey the writing set. His hope was that the writing set would keep her from forgetting him. The biggest laugh of the day was when Ocher got his present, a writing box. She also gave him a hand woven saddle blanket for the Pinto. The Double LL hands and Bug gave him hand tooled saddle bags.

Bug fussed over getting a present, saying "I'm beholden for a second chance," but didn't turn down the new Stetson. The Double LL hands were just as pleased with the big bags of hard candy. All in all, it was a good day except for the fact that Stacey would be leaving the next day.

It's time. The Sheriff looks at the Livingston's. "Best get started before this rain gets the creeks up and before the town realizes he's here," motioning toward Ocher. The stage driver moves from the boot of the coach and opens the passenger compartment door for Stacey. She walks to the hitching post and speaks to the Pinto. "Take good care of him," then turns and hugs her mom and dad. At the last moment she walks over to Ocher and kisses him on the cheek. The kiss so surprises Ocher that, before he can say anything he hears the door of the coach being shut. The driver steps up, grabs the reins and without any fanfare the coach is gone.

Ocher stands his ground for a moment more, then shakes Lewis's hand. For a second, he gets caught off guard with a hug and another kiss on the cheek from Amanda. The Pinto has had enough of this and stomps his right front hoof, pulls at the reins tied to the hitching post and snorts. Ocher gets the message, and, gives one last nod to the Livingston's, he steps into the saddle and rides out into the rain, adjusting his new lavender-scented bandana.

Coming soon –

Ocher's Wind
Ocher Jones Western Series –
Book Three

Ocher's Fire
Ocher Jones Western Series –
Book Four

Synopsis of Ocher's Wind -

During a violent dust storm, Ocher and the vaqueros from Tyler Gomez's ranch are ambushed. The horses, they are driving west, are stolen. Ocher sets off alone to recover the herd. He isn't alone for long. He finds an injured Apache boy, meets up with an old friend, and recovers the horses.

During his chase to recover the herd, the Pinto is stolen. His walk through the desert to El Paso, Texas reveals another secret, a noisy one.

Ocher's hope, that his life will become uneventful, is shattered when Holt shows up at the ranch, beaten almost to death, with a message.

We have Stacey, bring the jewels or she dies.

Contact information:

Mike Gipson

msguscg@gmail.com

Made in the USA
Middletown, DE
18 April 2025